"That was so much fun," Kamaya said, breaking the blanket of silence that had descended over them.

"It was fun. And you surprised me. You have serious dance skills."

"Five years of Latin dance lessons. You should see me rumba!"

Before Wesley could respond, a flash of white light burst in the sky above their heads. Kamaya grinned, clapping her hands together excitedly. She was giddy with excitement, her reaction almost childlike.

The lights continued to burst, fireworks snapping, crackling and popping with a vengeance. She shifted her body against his, the two of them settling comfortably against each other. Wesley draped an arm around her and pulled her close as she leaned her head against his shoulder. They both stared toward the darkened sky.

The fireworks exploded. The moment was enchanting, and Kamaya couldn't remember the last time she'd felt so carefree and relaxed.

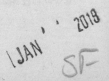

Dear Reader,

Who hasn't hid a secret from family and friends?
Well, Kamaya Boudreaux has some big secrets! And
I loved writing about every one of them. When the sexy
Wesley Walters gets tangled in her web of lies and deceit,
the two blend like fire and fire, igniting a blaze that will
keep you hanging on to the edge of your seat until the
very last word.

I really like this story! Breathing life into Kamaya's and
Wesley's characters came with some challenges, but the
research was all kinds of fun. From start to finish theirs
was a connection that just felt right.

A Pleasing Temptation is all about the power of love. How
deeply it cuts. How intensely it can pack a punch or
soothe an ache.

Kamaya and Wesley epitomize love that manifests when
it's least expected. Love is all things joyous and happy
and absolutely necessary!

Thank you so much for your continued support. I
am humbled by all the love you keep showing me, my
characters and our stories. I know that none of this
would be possible without you.

Until the next time, please take care, and may God's
blessings be with you always.

With much love,

Deborah Fletcher Mello

www.DeborahMello.Blogspot.com

A Pleasing Temptation

DEBORAH FLETCHER MELLO

HARLEQUIN® KIMANI™ ROMANCE

Recycling programs
for this product may
not exist in your area.

ISBN-13: 978-0-373-86493-5

A Pleasing Temptation

For questions and comments about the quality of this book please contact us at CustomerService@Harlequin.com.

HARLEQUIN®
www.Harlequin.com

Printed in U.S.A.

Having been writing since forever, **Deborah Fletcher Mello** can't imagine herself doing anything else. Her first novel, *Take Me to Heart*, earned her a 2004 Romance Slam Jam nomination for Best New Author. In 2008, Deborah won an RT Reviewers' Choice award for Best Series Romance for *Tame a Wild Stallion*. Deborah was also named the 2016 Romance Slam Jam Author of the Year. She has received accolades from several publications, including *Publishers Weekly*, *Library Journal*, and *RT Book Reviews*. With each new book, Deborah continues to create unique story lines and memorable characters. Born and raised in Connecticut, Deborah now considers home to be wherever the moment moves her.

Books by Deborah Fletcher Mello

Harlequin Kimani Romance

Promises to a Stallion

Seduced by a Stallion

Forever a Stallion

Passionate Premiere

Truly Yours

Hearts Afire

Twelve Days of Pleasure

My Stallion Heart

Stallion Magic

Tuscan Heat

A Stallion's Touch

A Pleasing Temptation

Visit the Author Profile page at Harlequin.com for more titles.

To my favorite Music Man, thank you for keeping that turntable spinning and that seductive beat burning. Dirty little secrets forever!

Chapter 1

"Finding a man has never been my problem," Kamaya Boudreaux mumbled under her breath as she exchanged a look with her older sister, who grinned. "I can find a man. A very large, well-endowed man!" Her tone was low, the comment meant for her sister's ears only. She winced when she realized her twin brother had happened to overhear.

"Ewww! Way too much information," Kendrick Boudreaux muttered, a deep frown pulling his full lips downward.

Kamaya shot him a look as she rolled her eyes.

The private jet had barely taken off before Kamaya was being interrogated by her parents about her personal life. Or lack thereof, depending on how you chose to look at it. Her family had just left Arizona where her parents had married off their youngest daughter. Now, they were suddenly focused on Kamaya, the only one of their nine children still unmarried. Both had had way too much to say. Kamaya shook her head and rolled her eyes a second time.

"You work too hard, Kamaya," Senior Boudreaux noted. "You can't find a man when you're always in that office by yourself!"

Kamaya took a deep breath. "I really don't, Senior. But aren't you the one who always told us to handle our business first? That all the rest could wait? That's exactly what I'm doing."

Obviously still giddy that her most pretentious child had gotten married in the most pragmatic manner, Katherine Boudreaux laughed. "She's not alone *all* the time, Senior. That Paxton boy is always sniffing around. Just waiting for Kamaya to show him some attention. Isn't that right, Kamaya?"

Laughter rang warmly through the space. Kamaya was beginning to wither under the parental assault, and her siblings seemed amused as she sank deeper into her leather seat. Beginning to look like a twelve-year-old under the scrutiny, it was clear she wasn't entertained by their conversation. Without some sibling intervention she knew the plane's landing would be her only saving grace from their old people's impromptu relationship intervention.

"Paxton's cool and all," Kendrick interjected, referring to Kamaya's friend and business partner, "but he's not right for Kamaya. You know anyone she dates has to pass my approval first, right? Can't have my twin with just anybody!"

"I know that's right!" their brother Darryl interjected. "Only the best for our girls!"

Their oldest sister, Maitlyn Sayed laughed. "Yeah, right! You boys used to get a kick out of scaring our guys away more than anything else. Just ask Tarah!"

"Tarah's glad we scared them off," Kendrick countered. "If we hadn't she wouldn't be Mrs. Nicholas Stallion. Knowing how she used to pick 'em, she'd be married to that guy with the crossed eye."

"I thought he had a squint eye," Katherine teased.

Kendrick shrugged. "Crossed, squint, whatever. He wasn't the right guy, either."

Kamaya released a soft sigh. "Well, I really appreciate all this family love and support but, really, I don't need any help right now. When I do, you all will be the first to know."

Her brothers and sisters all laughed as one of them changed the subject, reminiscing about everything that had been good and right about the wedding. Then their mother shifted the conversation back to Kamaya.

"Kamaya, have you thought about where you'd like to be married? Do you want a big wedding or small wedding?"

"Weren't you just pointing out that I needed to find a *groom*?" Kamaya said snidely. "Let's not put the cart before the horse. Isn't that one of your favorite mantras?" She paused. "You all really just need to leave me the hell alone!" she snapped.

Katherine cut an eye at Kamaya then, her stare noting her displeasure with Kamaya's curt tone.

The entire space went quiet, everyone holding a collective breath. A cloud of tension suddenly hung low enough to touch. Gazes skated back and forth between Kamaya and their parents, waiting to see who would jump first. Only the hum of the plane's engines sounded in the air.

Kamaya suddenly tensed, her eyes widening. "I didn't mean to say it like that," she mumbled, contrition furrowing her brow. Her eyes skipped from one of her parents to the other. Her father had shifted forward in his seat and her mother's jaw had locked tight as she sat with her arms folded over her chest. "I apologize. That was really rude of me."

Katherine nodded. "It was downright disrespectful and I expect better than that from you. From all of you! That's not how your daddy and I raised any of you kids."

"Don't let it happen again," Senior said matter-of-factly. "You *all* know how to speak to your mother like you got some sense! I won't tolerate any disrespect toward this woman and I don't care if you are in your feelings!"

"Yes, sir," Kamaya nodded. "I really am sorry." She turned her eyes toward her twin brother, suddenly wishing she could find a hole to crawl into. *Damn, how old am I?* she pondered, feeling very small under the scrutiny of her parents.

Kendrick wrapped her in a bear hug, laughing heartily. "It'll be all right, Yaya," he said, calling her by the pet name he'd used since they were two years old. "We all know you didn't mean it."

Kamaya gave her siblings a look. Deep down she had meant it, and each of them knew it. Maitlyn winked at her.

Feigning exhaustion, Kamaya shook herself from her brother's embrace. Rising from where she sat, she moved toward the rear of the luxury aircraft and claimed an empty window seat in the back corner. Waving a hand for the stewardess she asked for a blanket and a pillow. After covering herself from head to toe, she closed her eyes and pretended to fall asleep.

For another ten minutes her parents bemoaned her situation and then, just like that, the conversation stalled, everyone seeming to fall into their own thoughts. Kamaya welcomed the quiet, grateful that she was no longer the center of the unwanted attention. She was even more appreciative that no one had been able to read the emotion on her face as she, too, had suddenly wondered why there was no significant partner in her life.

A soft sigh eased past her lips as she snuggled deeper beneath the warmth of the blanket around her shoulders. Kamaya had never put much thought into her own happily-ever-after. She had always considered relationships that lasted longer than a minute to be an anomaly. For every one that seemed to be going well, she knew a dozen others that had imploded with a vengeance.

Kamaya had never imagined the perfect guy to grow old with, because she truly believed none existed. Even when her siblings had each fallen head over heels, one after the other, she'd waited with bated breath for the other shoe to fall on each of their relationships.

Her sister Katrina had been the first. She had been married, widowed, and left a single mother at a very young age. Her heartbreak had set the tone for what Kamaya never wanted to see in her own life. Then Katrina had been seduced by corporate attorney Matthew Stallion. One of four wealthy brothers out of Dallas, Texas, Matthew had swept Katrina off her feet. The two then married, and were now raising Katrina's son Collin and their own child, Matthew Jacoby Junior.

Their eldest brother, billionaire Mason Boudreaux III had been next, finding forever with the only Stallion sister, Phaedra. The two were now building another successful empire with their two sons Cole and Fletcher, and their daughter Addison.

Following on Mason's heels, their brother Guy had gotten a lifetime gig with filmmaker Dalia Morrow, their passionate premiere netting them five achievement awards: two sets of twins, Sydney and Cicely, and Zora and Langston, as well as their son Oscar. Their brother Darryl had been next. Truly his, Camryn Charles had designed their future from start to finish, their only daughter, Alexa, tossed into the mix.

Big sister Maitlyn, the second mother of the Boudreaux brood, had crashed and burned with her first marriage, but she'd actually tried it again, her heart afire for Zakaria Sayed, the very best friend of Kamaya's twin, Kendrick. Maitlyn and Zakaria's daughter, Rose-Lynn, son, Zayn, and a baby yet to be named, had the couple making up for much lost time.

Kendrick had never been interested in a long-term relationship, and was solely focused on his top-secret career. On the subject of marriage, the twins had seen eye to eye. Then Kendrick had gotten himself lost for twelve days of pleasure with a client. Vanessa Harrison had been his dream come true, and when he'd finally come up for air, he, too, had been ready to walk down the matrimonial aisle.

Even the most conservative of the Boudreaux siblings, the son everyone had sworn would be the last to marry with him being so committed to his career, had beaten Kamaya to the altar. Their brother Donovan had flown around the world to the Tuscan heat chasing his dream. Now he and renowned author Gianna Martelli were writing their own love story as they awaited the birth of their first child.

And now, with Tarah, the baby of the family, suddenly someone's missus, Kamaya found herself on the hook, everyone anxious for her to catch and reel in her own happy ending. But, truth be told, despite all that happy everyone in her family claimed to be having, Kamaya just wasn't willing to trust any man with her heart.

Maitlyn dropped into the seat beside her. "You good?" she asked, concern ringing in her loud whisper.

Kamaya nodded. "Yeah, I'm fine." She lifted her eye toward her parents who were huddled in conversation. "They still mad at me?"

"They weren't mad. Mom's just worried. You know how she is. And you snapping at her didn't help. Now she's even more concerned about you."

"I didn't mean for that to happen. It just slipped."

"Yeah, you were being a little sensitive. Do you want to talk about it?"

Kamaya shrugged. "Not really. I'm just ready to get back to work. I need to focus on something other than bridal gowns and floral arrangements."

Maitlyn giggled softly. "It really wasn't that bad. And how beautiful was our little sister?"

"She was stunning. It's so strange to see Tarah all grown-up and mature-like. Nicholas has been good for her."

"She's been good for Nicholas. And your turn is coming."

Kamaya scoffed. "Did anyone ever think I might not *want* a turn?"

Maitlyn nodded. "I did. But your mother says differently, and you know Katherine Toutant Boudreaux is never wrong about anything!"

"You got that right!" their mother interjected. She had moved down the aisle and was suddenly standing beside them.

Kamaya smiled. "You still love me?"

Katherine waved a dismissive hand at her. "Don't I always?"

The three women smiled brightly at each other. Their ensuing conversation was calm and easy, Kamaya falling back into balance with everyone.

The flight attendant interrupted the moment. "Ma'am, the pilot is preparing the plane for landing. We'll need you to take a seat and put your seat belt on, please."

Katherine nodded, hesitating for one minute longer. "Are you coming to the house after we land?" she asked, meeting Kamaya's stare.

Kamaya shook her head. "I don't think so. I really need to stop in at the office and check on things, and then I want to go home and catch up on some sleep."

Her mother nodded. "Plan on lunch next week. I need to make sure you're really okay."

Kamaya smiled, exchanging a look with her sister. "Yes, ma'am."

"Yes, ma'am. I will. Yes, ma'am." Wesley Leroy Walters was nodding into his cell phone.

On the other end, his mother, Annie Walters was cataloging a lengthy list of must-dos and expectations. "And I want you to get to church sometime soon," the older woman said.

His father laughed, chiming in on their three-way

conversation. "God knows your heart, son! Just do a drive by, wave at the pastor and get back to work. Jesus will excuse you."

"Leon Walters! How are you going to tell our son some foolishness like that!" Annie exclaimed.

His father laughed and Wesley laughed with him. He could just imagine the look on his poor mother's face. It made him smile as he thought about the only woman in the world who had his whole heart.

"It's all good, Ma. I promise I'll go to service this Sunday," Wesley said. Behind him, the sound system suddenly blasted on, the throbbing techno bass of the 1983 club hit "White Horse" echoing throughout the room. It surprised him, his eyes widening as he slammed his palm against the mouthpiece of his cell phone.

"Wesley, what's that noise?" his mother questioned, the sound carrying over the phone line.

"Sorry!" he exclaimed, as he shot a look at the sound man in the corner, gesturing for him to turn the music down. "I turned on my radio and didn't realize the volume was so high," he said, the little white lie spilling past his full lips.

His father chuckled. "Thought you all were having a party in that office of yours."

"No. No. Nothing like that," Wesley said as he shot an evil eye toward the other men in the room. "But I do have to run," he said. "I need to get ready for a meeting. I'll give you a call tomorrow, okay?"

"Of course, baby," his mother answered.

"Handle your business, son!" his father added.

After telling them both that they were loved, Wesley disconnected the call. "What the hell?" he shouted over the music.

On the stage, Bryan Lackey was refining his dance routine. He gave Wesley a thumbs-up as he gyrated his hips from side to side.

Trey Jackson laughed. "You know he did that on purpose, right?"

Wesley shook his head. "I swear, if one of you outs me to my mother there's going to be hell to pay!"

The other men in their group laughed heartily and Wesley couldn't help but laugh along with them.

Bryan turned off the music and jumped down from the stage. "Sorry about that, big guy. I didn't know it was your mother. I just knew you were lying to some stray you picked up here at the club."

"When the hell have you known Mr. Straight-As-An-Arrow to pick up anyone from the club?" Trey asked.

Bryan shrugged. "There's a first time for everything," he said casually.

"You do know who you're talking about right?"

The group laughed.

Wesley shook his head. Standing among his closest friends in the world, the men he'd known for too many years to count, he trusted them with his secrets. Knowing not one would ever purposely betray him, he also knew that any of them would take great pleasure at an opportunity to make him sweat.

Since his sophomore year at Grambling State, the men in that room had stood by him, offering a friendship that felt more like a family bond. He and Bryan had met first, college roommates. Biracial, Bryan had been the only blue-eyed blond with a porcelain complexion in their dorm. As much as he stood out, he'd fit in, and they'd become fast friends.

Trey Jackson had been their fraternity brother, pushing them both to pledge Kappa Alpha Psi. When the trio had bemoaned the stresses of financial aid or lack thereof, Victor Hudson had come with an answer to all their problems. Wesley remembered that defining moment as if it had just happened yesterday.

The party they'd been invited to had been a Who's Who of Louisiana's finest. A smorgasbord of beautiful, sexy, financially successful women looking for a night of entertainment. Before either Wesley or Trey could change their minds, someone had turned on the music, each had been given a stage name and the rest had been history. They had all started dancing to supplement their empty pockets. Now they each continued for a variety of reasons. Together, they were the hottest male exotic dance troupe to grace the state.

Bryan "The White Prince" Lackey, Trey "Hammer" Jackson, and Victor "Black Magic" Hudson were Wesley's closest friends and they made up both the senior management team and talent at his newest venture: The Wet Bar. The newly purchased franchise was destined to be the hottest nightclub in New Orleans.

He turned toward his office. "Joke all you want. Being straight-as-an-arrow has kept me out of all sorts of trouble. You three should try it sometime."

"Like that would be fun," Victor quipped, and then turned the music back on.

Inside his office Wesley blew out a heavy breath as he dropped into his leather executive chair. Despite his joviality with his boys, he hated lying to his parents.

Keeping secrets from them hurt his heart. It wasn't how he'd been raised and it wasn't at all indicative of the man he strove to be. But neither Leon nor Annie Walters would approve of his endeavors in the adult entertainment market. Although he knew his father would wink and make a joke about his situation, he also knew his mother would be mortified. And that's why he had never bothered to tell them.

Dancing hadn't been Wesley's career of choice. It had been a means to an end, and with that goal just at his fingertips he could appreciate it for all it had been. He had preferred being called an exotic dancer, but in the adult entertainment industry stripping was what he had done. Stripping had helped pay for his bachelor's degree in business management and his master's in finance. And it was currently helping him purchase this franchise.

He aspired to be a corporate mogul, running his own multi-million-dollar business and The Wet Bar was just the beginning. He had danced to pay the bills and dancing had afforded him the opportunity to save and invest the money he'd made. The Wet Bar franchise was a viable business opportunity and he planned to transform and legitimize the business, making it the most talked-about venture in an industry some considered tawdry and decadent. Renovating the New Orleans location was just the beginning. He then hoped to purchase additional franchises and expand to multiple cities throughout the nation.

Despite his efforts to hide what he did from his family, there was no hiding that he knew the business like the back of his hand. He knew how to grow the client base and how to give them what they wanted. Stripping didn't begin to define the entertainment business that would become the cornerstone of his empire.

The office door opened and the echo of Lady Gaga's "Poker Face" vibrated through the entrance. Bryan poked his head into the room. "Hey, you busy?"

Wesley shook his head. "No. Just trying to figure out what comes next. Come on in," he said, as he gestured for his friend to take a seat. "What's up?"

"We got a call from the corporate office. A local television news show is doing a profile piece on the company and since our renovations are almost done, they'd like to film here."

"Here?"

Bryan nodded, a wide grin spreading like spilled sugar across his face. "They said they'd like to spotlight you and your goals for the business. They thought it would be a good idea to showcase the grand reopening to help promote the place."

"Wow! That's...wow!"

Bryan laughed. "That's what I said. They're going to send some folks from their executive team to scout the place, talk to you and make sure it's all a good fit for what they're looking to accomplish."

Wesley took a deep breath. "When?"

"They'll be here tomorrow at noon."

A loud expletive blew harshly out of his mouth. "I need to talk to the contractor. We have to be done on time. We can't blow this."

Bryan winked. "I grabbed him earlier and told him to come see you before he leaves."

Wesley nodded his appreciation. "This is really happening."

"Man! You're about to blow up!"

Chapter 2

"You look like you just got off a plane," Paxton Reid said, his gaze sweeping the length of Kamaya's slim frame.

"So now you have jokes? You know I just got off an airplane." She was wearing oversized sweatpants, a tank top and Converse sneakers. The look was too casual and very basic.

"But you look like you just flew on a commercial flight and not private. You should look way better."

"You're an ass," Kamaya said, narrowing her gaze on the man. She and Paxton Reid had been best friends for years. They'd met in high school, lab partners who both hated science with a passion. For a brief moment they'd been a couple, but that hadn't worked. Occasionally they were lovers, and that did work, even when it didn't. Despite their obvious differences—he was white and a male—they genuinely cared about each other and most days that was more than enough.

Her eyes rolled as she took the short flight of stairs to the front entrance of her office space. The Michelle Initiatives, located on Lee Street, was welcoming and looked like they were in the business of selling cupcakes and lollipops. The old two-story home with its lime-colored paint, bright yellow shutters and red door belied what was really happening behind the wooden entrance.

Kamaya had named the business after herself. Michelle was her middle name. Her brother Mason had the monopoly on their last name, Boudreaux Enterprises being his claim to fame. Michelle had been personal enough, but not so much that it drew any unwanted attention from her family. Because The Michelle Initiative was all about adult entertainment.

Most of Kamaya's businesses, either directly or indirectly, provided sex-related products and services to an adult clientele. On the titillating side there was Play Candy, her line of adult sex toys, Eye Candy, the adult publishing line that was home to erotic stories, and her newest acquisition, forty-three strip clubs across the country soon to be renamed "The Wet Bar" and revitalized to cater to an upscale female clientele. On the less sensationalistic side there were the upscale massage parlors, A Touch Above, and the vaginal rejuvenation centers, Secret Garden Clinics. But, when asked, all Kamaya ever talked about were the convenience stores and gas stations that had been the foundation of her expanding portfolio. In the corporate offices of The Michelle Initiative she employed a staff of thirty-six people who all operated out of the pretty, gingerbread-trimmed home.

Paxton bounded up the steps behind her. "I may be an ass but I'm an honest ass!" he said, his expression smug. "And you can always trust me to tell you the truth!"

Kamaya tossed him a look as she pushed her way inside. "So what have I missed?" she asked.

"The first Wet Bar franchise is opening soon. Renovations are almost done and we meet with the franchise owner tomorrow."

"Is he on board for the feature?" she asked. "He understands that we want him to be the face of The Wet Bar?"

"Well, he will. I figured we'd break the news to him in person."

Kamaya's eyes widened. "You told me we weren't going to have any problems. You know very well that you and I can't be associated…"

"I told you. It's not a problem. No one will ever connect your good family name with the business."

Disaster suddenly flashed before Kamaya's eyes as she imagined everything going straight to hell. She suddenly had visions of her parents disowning her and her siblings disavowing any knowledge of who she was. People discovering that she was hawking sex and not chips and beer could be potentially devastating. She slapped her palm against the desktop. "I knew this wasn't a good idea. I don't know why I let you talk me into doing this profile piece."

"I've got this! And we need the exposure. If we're going to sell these franchises and grow this brand you need to do this."

Before Kamaya could respond, their secretary, Virginia Wade, called her name, purposely interrupting the conversation. The two were renowned for their no blows held back battles and a rise of ire was beginning to curdle like spoiled milk between them. "Kamaya, I left some checks on your desk to be signed, and the massage center called to confirm your appointment. You need to be there by eight tomorrow morning." The woman smiled. "And welcome back."

"Thank you, Virginia," Kamaya said as she moved from the reception area into her office space. She pointed her index finger in Paxton's direction. "I swear, if this blows up…"

"It won't. Stop worrying, please. We've been doing this for how many years now? No one has discovered anything about your salacious endeavors and they never will."

The two exchanged a look and then she closed the door behind her as Paxton stood on the other side.

There weren't enough hours in a day to do everything Kamaya needed to do. She was past the point of exhaustion and she still had a grocery list of things that she needed. Work had moved from her office to the dining room in her Marengo Street home. She pushed the folders from in front of her to the other side of her table, shifting documents from point A to point B as she attempted to bring some organization to the mess.

She had bought the chain of strip clubs in spite of having some reservations, but the purchase price had been too good to pass up. Envisioning where she could take the down-and-out titty bars had been a no-brainer. Revamping their programs, revitalizing their interior designs and hiring all male dancers had been the easiest decision to make. There was a market eager to enjoy the adult entertainment men brought to the dance stage. Women loved watching beautiful, hard-bodied males and they were willing to pay well for the privilege.

Franchising the properties and the business formula had been Kamaya's idea. Starting with the New Orleans's property had been Paxton's, the proximity of the location allowing them an up close and personal view of what would work and what would not. That, and his inside connection to the investor who'd easily come up with the required cash had been enough for her to trust her old friend with the reins. Now she was excited to see if he'd actually been able to pull off her vision.

She pushed herself from the table and stole a quick glance at the clock on the wall. It was just past midnight and although she knew she needed some rest, she was anxious, her entire body a ball of nerves. She needed release. Something heated and dirty, where sweat carried the fretfulness from her body. She needed her sure thing for just an hour, or maybe even two if it was really good. In the realm of Kamaya's small world, men were toys, sex was a game and she knew how to play them both to her advantage.

As she moved toward the master bedroom she pulled her cell phone from her back pocket and pushed the speed-dial button. Paxton answered on the third ring.

"Why are you still up?" he asked, his voice low, as if he were whispering.

"I have a lot on my mind," Kamaya noted. "Is this a bad time?"

There was a moment of hesitation before he answered. "Can we talk in the morning?"

A hint of surprised lifted her brow. "Oh, I'm sorry. I didn't mean…"

"It's no big deal," he said cutting her off. "Laney just stopped by. She was upset and then she fell asleep…"

"Laney?"

He took a deep breath. "I was going to tell you tomorrow. Actually I was planning on telling you today but, well…" He took another inhale of air. "I asked Laney to marry me and she said yes. We're getting married."

Kamaya paused, his words seeming to go in one ear and explode someplace deep in her head. "You and Laney are getting married?"

"I really hope you'll be happy for us, Kamaya. You're my best friend, and it's important to me that…"

She interrupted him. "Let's talk tomorrow," she said and then, just like that, she disconnected the call.

Seconds later the device rang, vibrating in the palm of her hand as an image of her and Paxton together flashed across the screen. She pushed the power button, and when the phone was off she tossed it to the floor of her walk-in closet and slammed the door shut.

Something like rage teased her spirit. She was surprised by Paxton's news and she shouldn't have been. Laney McDonald had been his Achilles' heel for too many years to count. The woman had been blowing in and out of his life like a wayward wind, restless and wandering and never making any significant impact while there.

Laney McDonald was why she and Paxton had never been able to take their relationship past the point of friendship with occasional benefits. His obsession with the green-eyed redhead was like a fungus that had taken hold and refused to be eradicated. Laney would always find the most inopportune moments to suddenly come calling, teary eyed and emotional over something that had gone wrong and fallen apart in her life. She was a damsel in perpetual distress, and Kamaya's buddy and pal Paxton felt obligated to save her.

Each time Laney needed to be handled, Paxton went running. Each time Kamaya's feelings had been hurt for a split second. Deep down she knew that there would never be anything more between them and that she and Paxton would forever be friends.

Even their sexual connection had been a fluke of sorts, a night of too much rum and not enough cola spinning them into bed together. It would never have happened again if Paxton's skills between the sheets hadn't been so mind-blowing, but her friend was damn good in bed!

After that Kamaya had used him to scratch that itch when she didn't want to be bothered with someone else. Because the someone else was always wanting more from her than she was willing to give. Paxton had been convenient and since she didn't want permanent, it had worked for them both. And now he was planning to marry Laney. Kamaya couldn't help but wonder what Laney's husband had to say about it all.

For too many years Paxton had gone after the very married, very wealthy socialite like a rat chasing cheese. Sometimes he had stooped to a new low that had her questioning his sanity. But through it all Kamaya had known the two were a disaster waiting to happen. She was just glad she would be far from the mix when they exploded.

Stripping out of her clothes she moved from her bedroom into the bathroom. She reached for the faucet and turned on the water. She needed a shower. And she needed it ice cold.

* * *

It was close to two in the morning when Wesley locked the doors to the club and headed to his house on Camp Street. The custom home was centered in a prime location near Audubon Park. Wesley had been drawn to the home's warm and charming simplicity. He'd first seen it when the market was down, homes lingering for months in the For Sale directory. He had considered it a blessing when he discovered the house was still on the market when he'd finally had the money to buy it outright.

Inside, he paused as he took in the herringbone brick floors and the wide planked pine that ran through the foyer and living room. During the daylight hours there was lots of natural light and everything about the space felt welcoming. The decor was extremely sparse; a futon and some pillows sat off to the side in the living room and there were a small table and two chairs in the kitchen. In the master bedroom, a king-sized mattress and box spring sat on the floor. It wasn't much, but it was his and his chest swelled with pride each time he stepped through the door.

For a brief moment Wesley thought about making dinner, but he found the prospect of having to cook something daunting. Standing in front of the refrigerator he marveled that, for the first time in a long time, there was absolutely no leftovers inside. Deciding he wasn't that hungry, he grabbed a Budweiser and the last of a bag of Cheetos from the counter and headed up to his bedroom.

He was excited about the future and he knew he was just hours from another turning point that would take him toward his goals. He'd been working hard to insure that The Wet Bar set the standard for those that would come after. He planned on owning as many of them as he could.

Lying across his bed he knew that he wouldn't be able to keep what he did from his parents for much longer. But if all went according to plan, by the time they discovered the truth it wouldn't make a difference. He'd be running an empire, making them proud of his success and accomplishments. Wesley had big dreams.

He suddenly realized how quiet his home was. Nothing creaked or leaked or gave him any reason to pause. It was disconcerting, and for the first time in a long time he felt very alone. He blew a soft sigh as he swallowed the last cheesy snack and then sat up to toss the crumpled wrapper into the trash. After chugging back the last of his bottled beer he threw his body back across the mattress.

For a brief moment he pondered the women he could invite to come spend some time with him. The list of late-night booty calls he could make at that hour was probably lengthy, but that kind of company really wasn't what he wanted. As he thought about his future he knew he didn't want to do casual with any woman. That time in his life had come and gone. He wanted more and he would only have the best. He prayed that God knew his needs and would bless him abundantly.

Rising, he moved himself from his bedroom into the shower. He came out of his clothes along the way, leaving a trail behind him. Stepping into the enclosure, he dashed his head beneath the hot water and allowed the spray to pelt his back. The heated moisture was soothing as it massaged him gently. He thought again about the women who were in his life. Or, more honestly, the women who weren't.

Wesley couldn't remember the last time he'd gone on a second or a third date. But he'd had more than his fair share of first and last dates. He was used to women throwing themselves at him. More times than he cared to count, women who had seen him perform or who knew what he used to do saw him as little more than a slab of beef, good for a late night between the sheets.

Brenda-Joy Taylor had been the closest thing to a serious relationship that he'd ever had. She'd been a church-going girl and someone his mother had liked. They had grown up together, and both their families had assumed the two would end up married with kids.

But Brenda-Joy hadn't wanted the same life he had yearned for. She'd been happy with average and regular and hadn't aspired to do anything extraordinary. The day she'd told him his dreams were too big had been the beginning of the end for them. He dreamed too big and she didn't dream at all.

The last he'd heard, Brenda-Joy had married Quadell Baker. Quadell was an aspiring rapper, unemployed and sometimes known to stand on street corners, asking for handouts to help support her and their five kids. Apparently Quadell didn't do much dreaming, either. But Wesley aspired to greatness and he couldn't fathom a life of anything less.

The exterior of The Wet Bar was basic, at best; nothing about it raised any red flags. Despite its proximity to Bourbon Street and the French Quarter, there was nothing about the building or parking lot that drew anyone's attention as to what might be happening be-

hind its doors. It was exactly what Kamaya wanted; the
neon lights and abrasive signs that had been there just
months ago were long gone. The women who would
frequent the club weren't interested in everyone knowing their business. Discretion was key and Kamaya had
insisted on everything that would make the clientele
comfortable.

She nodded approvingly as she sat in the club's parking lot waiting for Paxton to arrive. The two hadn't spoken since he'd delivered the news that he was tying the
knot. If canceling had been an option, she would have,
knowing that at some point her friend would want to
talk about his marriage plans and she wasn't interested
in having that conversation with him.

She still couldn't fathom what all the fuss was about.
In her humble opinion marriage was an antiquated con-
cept pushed by bible-thumping radicals, the Hallmark
greeting-card industry, bridal bloggers and her parents. Intelligent, educated women didn't need a ring
and a license to legitimize their most intimate relationships. They could build empires, mother babies and still
enjoy the love of a good man. Oprah was doing it with
Stedman, Coco Chanel had enjoyed the Duke of West-
minster, Sheryl Crow had her lengthy list of talented,
wealthy, successful male companions. Even Simone de
Beauvoir and the existentialist philosopher Sartre had
made love work without marriage. Marriage worked
for some but Kamaya couldn't ever see herself doing it.

Her thoughts shifted as she watched a car pull into an
empty parking space right at the door. This one caught
her attention and held it because the vehicle was neither
flashy nor pretentious. It was a drastic contrast to the
other vehicles sitting in the lot. She'd been watching as

one dancer after another in some high-priced, high-end vehicle, wearing low-slung jeans or sweats and looking like they'd just graduated from a semester of thugs-are-us paraded into the club. They'd been hard bodied and buff and some very entertaining eye candy.

But this car and its owner were in a class all to themselves. The hooptie had seen better days, rust and Bondo holding it together. After shutting down the engine the driver continued to sit, seeming to look for something that had fallen between the seats. As he finally stepped out of the vehicle and locked the car door with the key, she eyed him curiously.

The tailored suit he wore looked like silk. The classic styling fit him to perfection, and unlike his car, his clothes looked expensive. The suit was a charcoal gray and he'd paired it with a white dress shirt, a somber gray and black print necktie and black dress shoes that were polished to a high gloss. He looked very corporate and very boring. Had she dressed him, he would have worn a hint of color, maybe a lavender shirt, something that hinted at a semblance of personality. Assuming he had a personality.

For a brief moment he looked toward her car, but she knew he couldn't see inside the darkly tinted windows. Which was a good thing, because as his curious gaze skated in her direction, Kamaya felt a wave of heat course through her body and tinge her cheeks a deep shade of red.

Whoever he was, he was quite good-looking. Exceptionally good-looking! His complexion was a deep, warm vat of smooth, melted chocolate. His chiseled features were a testament to good genes, and even with the barest hint of a smile pulling at his full lips there was no missing the deep wells that dimpled his cheeks. He had facial hair, his beard and mustache meticulously edged and trimmed. He was better than good-looking and Kamaya was suddenly wanting to know more about the tall, dark and handsome stranger.

Just as he turned, moving through the front door of the building, Paxton pulled into the space beside her, his toothy grin wide, his blond locks stylishly unkempt. He stole a glance toward his wristwatch as he jumped from his car.

"Hey!" he exclaimed as he pulled her car door open. "Sorry. I had to get Laney situated before I could leave. Good morning!"

Kamaya gave him one of her infamous looks, her eyes narrowed ever so slightly, her jaw tight, her teeth clenched. There was no missing that she had no intentions of talking about his problems or his girlfriend. "We're still early," she said matter-of-factly. "Who are we meeting again?" She headed toward the building's front door, Paxton hurrying after her.

"His name is Walters. Wesley Walters. As well as this night club, he has optioned the next ten franchises based on our guaranteeing support and backing as defined in our initial contract. With a few exceptions."

"What few exceptions?"

"Nothing major. He'd like some concessions and control with how the business will evolve as a whole. It's not much more than what we've already talked about."

"And the things we haven't talked about?"

"They're things he's willing to back with a cash investment, if necessary."

"You mean, if he wants them badly enough."

Paxton nodded. "Yes."

Kamaya paused, her hand on the doorknob. She cut her eyes in Paxton's direction. "And you agreed to those things?"

"I agreed to discuss it with the both of you in order to come to a mutually beneficial agreement. The contracts I had drawn up detail what I think is in our best interest under the circumstances. He may ask for more. I don't know."

"How do you know this man again?"

"We met in graduate school. He's an upstanding guy. He's going to do big things with or without us."

Kamaya eyed Paxton a split second longer before finally giving him a quick nod, then she turned and moved into the club's inner sanctum.

Chapter 3

Wesley was standing in the center of the elevated stage pointing at the lights overhead. Lighting was key to every performance and he wasn't happy with the current luminosity. He was certain a change in the bulbs would solve the issue and he wanted to make it happen before the corporate franchisor showed up. The contractor was adjusting the last unit when Wesley spied Kamaya and Paxton entering the space.

His eyes widened as the stunning young woman moved in his direction. She was long and lean, with legs that seemed to go on for days. She wore black suede boots that stopped thigh high and a black leather skirt that stopped at her knees and zipped up the front. The zipper was open just high enough to allow a hint of thigh to show. Her sweater was black and long sleeved with a scooped neckline that showed off a hint of cleavage. With her hair loose, falling to her shoulders in soft, wavy curls and the barest hint of makeup on her face, she was gorgeous.

The fluidity of her movements was stealth-like, her eyes darted back and forth like a cheetah assessing prey. She'd gauged the space, the staff and him in one easy sweep around the room. From the expression on her face he sensed that she wasn't unhappy; just the barest hint of a smile pulled at her mouth and teased the gleam in her eyes. Everything about the woman was commanding, drawing the attention of every man in the room.

Stepping off the platform Wesley extended his hand in greeting. "Hello! I'm Wesley Walters."

"It's a pleasure to meet you, Mr. Walters. I'm Kamaya Boudreaux," she said, as she noted the warmth of his hand, the slightly calloused palm and the firmness of his grip. He met the look she was giving him with one of his own, his eyes skating across her face, and as their gazes connected heat erupted from deep in her abdomen. She took a step back, her eyes shifting far from his as her partner stepped up to greet the man.

Paxton shook Wesley's hand, the two men bumping shoulders in a gesture of familiarity. "It's good to see you again, Wes!"

"Paxton, how've you been?"

"I'm very good. And we're very excited to be working with you."

Wesley nodded, shooting Kamaya another look. "So, Ms. Boudreaux, how long have you owned…"

"I don't," she said, interrupting the question she felt coming. "We just represent the owner's interests. We *work* for The Michelle Initiative," she said, the little white lie spilling easily past her lips as her stare gestured toward Paxton.

"Oh, my apologies. I misunderstood." Wesley nodded. "Well, why don't we take this conversation to my office," he said.

"Why don't you give us a tour and update us with the status of your renovations," Kamaya ordered. Her tone was brusque and all business. She turned and moved toward the bar area, her gaze still dancing from pillar to post.

The two men cut their eyes at each other. Paxton shrugged "I report to her," he muttered under his breath.

Wesley nodded in understanding as he turned to follow the beautiful woman. "Structurally, we're done with the renovations. There are some minor issues with the tile in the women's restrooms that need to be addressed and I'm assured that they'll be resolved before end of business today. We are on schedule for our last inspection tomorrow and I anticipate we'll have our certificate of occupancy immediately after.

"Tables and chairs will be delivered later this week and the bar will be in place this weekend. The sound system and kitchen are all up and ready, and the interior designer will be here on Monday to add the final decorative touches to all of our guest spaces. We have a team of sixteen dancers who are ready to go at a moment's notice and our waitstaff will have three days of orientation training early next week. We are on schedule to open doors next month to a by-invitation-only crowd, and I'm confident that we will open to much success." He took a breath and then he continued.

"All the plans are detailed with respect to the decor and staffing if you'd like to review them. I've also printed out the budget and my preliminary forecasts. The numbers are good. They're even better than what I projected in my initial business plan."

Kamaya gave him a slight nod of her head. "It sounds like you have everything under control, Mr. Walters."

"Please, call me Wesley or Wes. Mr. Walters is my father."

Kamaya smiled. His thick Southern accent was deep and rich, only lacking the soundtrack to make his words as sultry as country crooner Chris Young's love songs.

The two were suddenly interrupted as Bryan Lackey moved between them. "Hey there, sorry to interrupt," he said, his grin canyon wide, "but the guys are ready when you are, boss man."

Wesley smiled. "Kamaya Boudreaux, Bryan Lackey. Bryan, Ms. Boudreaux is a member of the franchise team. She's here checking that we're ready to go next month."

Bryan nodded. "It's a pleasure. And I think we're definitely good to go. I'd love to show you our best."

"Bryan is our lead choreographer as well as my club manager."

Kamaya cut her eyes back and forth between the two men. "Then I'd love to see your best," she said, crossing her arms over her chest.

Bryan looked to Wesley for his approval, and then, with a nod of his head, he moved toward the stage, gesturing for the dance team to follow.

"Would you like a seat?" Wesley asked. "I can have a chair brought out from my office for you."

Kamaya shook her head as she shifted her weight from one hip to the other. "That's not necessary. But I appreciate the offer."

Wesley stared at her for a brief moment and then he gestured, pointing an index finger toward the stage.

Music suddenly echoed from every corner of the room. The acoustics were great, clearly demonstrating that some serious attention had been given to the sound system. Kamaya nodded her approval as she suddenly felt her whole body begin to sway with the beat. She didn't know the song but it had a lush, sexy vibe and she knew a female audience would instantly be engaged. And then the dance team strutted onto the stage.

Kamaya felt her heart skip a beat and then two. She took a step forward as if moving closer would give her a better view when she had the best line of sight in the house, nothing obscuring the stage. The next ten minutes, with three song changes, left Kamaya sweating, perspiration puddling in her creases and crevices as if someone had turned on an inner water faucet and left the water running.

There were twelve men on stage, each one a sight to behold. They all had bodies that were solid steel beneath baby smooth skin, six-pack abs and male model looks. They were a rainbow of hues from the darkest chocolate to the warmest vanilla. They were Black, Caucasian, Latino, Asian and a multitude of mixed races that had them looking like a United Nation's contingent.

When they were all standing in matching blue and green Speedos, hips and legs moving in near perfect sync as they gyrated to the deep, ravishing beat of the Black Eyed Peas' "Boom Boom Pow," an actual smile appeared on Kamaya's face.

Paxton leaned over her shoulder and whispered in her ear. "Down, girl!"

"Boy, bye!" Kamaya chuckled. She shot Wesley a

look, the man still staring at her. "Very impressive. You should all be very proud."

Wesley grinned. "Thank you. We are. Would you like to see an individual routine? Any of the guys would be willing to perform."

"That's not necessary," she said, shaking herself out of the reverie she'd fallen into. "I would like to know how you plan to keep things from becoming too raunchy, in order to establish an upscale image. We do want to maintain a semblance of decorum."

"None of the dancers will ever expose himself. They will go down to an approved G-string and some penis socks on the main stage, but definitely no full nudity. The costumes are top-notch, well made and artistically engineered. We also have procedures in place for any women who might get out of hand and want to get a little too touchy-feely."

Kamaya nodded her approval.

Wesley gestured for her to follow as he led them past the stage into the employees-only area. The men were all gathered, waiting to hear from him how well they'd done and if they'd made the powers in charge happy. As she passed, she paused for a split second, giving them all a thumbs-up and a wink. He tossed his friends a look but his attention was focused on Kamaya. He ushered her past the dressing area down a short hallway to another area of the building. Past the closed door was a row of tastefully decorated rooms, each with an oversized recliner, a settee, a coffee table and a pole.

"This was here with the original business," Wesley said. "There's another more private entrance at the opposite end of the hallway where we came in. It's now our VIP area for private dances for women wanting something more up close and personal. Women who are willing to pay for that discretion."

"We are not promoting prostitution!" Kamaya exclaimed, her incredulous expression moving him to smile. "There will be no happy ending rooms for you and your staff! That's not happening!"

He shook his head. "No, we are definitely not promoting prostitution and every dancer knows that they will be automatically dismissed if they ever engage in any kind of sexual activity on club premises in exchange for payment. Although what they do after they're off the clock is not our business and we can't control it. But there are women willing to pay well for some one-on-one attention. It's usually that uptight business executive who has to maintain an image even when she's here, but relishes an opportunity to get buck wild when no one is looking. You know the type. Women much like yourself."

Paxton laughed out loud at the comment. Kamaya gave him and Wesley a narrowed gaze.

Wesley smiled. "I apologize. That was out of order, but I was only teasing. Trying to lighten the mood."

There was a hint of amusement in Kamaya's eyes as her gaze danced with his. She blinked it away, shifting back to serious. "Do not get us shut down by the police's vice department because your men can't keep their dicks in their pants. And I mean it. If that ever happens, you may come up short in more ways than one. We are building a brand and an image, and I will not see that tarnished. I don't think you have a clue what's at stake."

Wesley's stance tensed, his shoulders pulling back as he seemed to grow taller where he stood. He took a step forward, meeting her toe to toe. He stared down into her eyes. "Don't get it twisted, Ms. Boudreaux, I am fully invested in the success of The Wet Bar. Now, I understand that the franchisor dictates the framework, the basics, but past that, I'm in charge. I'm managing and growing this business. I hire. I fire. I'll figure out what works and what doesn't. And I'll dictate how to market and promote every one of *my* locations. I'm wagering everything I have on making this model work for every franchise that comes after this one. Since I know that you and your bosses want to see me succeed, it will be a win–win situation for all. The *happy ending* rooms for our female *clientele* will stay."

The moment was suddenly tense, the air fraught with energy. The two stood, staring each other in the eye, falling headfirst into the look the other was giving. Each could have easily gotten lost in the other's gaze. Kamaya suddenly realized that she was panting slightly, the air thick and warm between them. She took a step back, wishing for a cool breeze to blow her out of the reverie she'd somehow managed to trip into. She decided to change the subject, ignoring his last comment.

"We're putting a significant amount of money into your marketing program over the next six weeks to support your grand opening. I reviewed your advertising campaign and it's been approved but…" She paused as she gestured for Paxton to pass her a manila folder from his briefcase. "It's my understanding that you may have worked with a dancer we think should be invited to help motivate the customers and help bring in a crowd. I'm told he was extremely popular and had quite a following. His stage name was Deuce or Deuces, but we haven't been able to find out anything else about him."

"Deuce?" Wesley's face suddenly went blank, his expression unreadable.

She nodded. "He had quite a reputation," she said, as she flipped through a number of newspaper articles. "But we haven't been able to find any photos or videos. Seems like he peaked prior to everything being captured on the internet, but the women are still talking about him. If he's dancing, maybe hire him to be a featured guest performer. If not, maybe he can MC or something. Either way, we think it'll be good for business."

"Maybe one of the other guys knows who he is?" Paxton interjected.

"Who?" Bryan questioned, having entered the room behind them. He looked from one to the other. "I'm sorry. I didn't mean to interrupt but the contractor needs you to take a look at the tile in the ladies' room." He tossed Wesley a nod. "So, who is it you want to know about?"

"A dancer by the name of Deuce," Paxton said. "Unfortunately, we don't have his government name."

"Deuce?" A slow smile pulled at the man's thin lips. "I know Deuce. I know him really well. In fact, he's a very good friend…"

"Well then," Wesley interrupted. "We know who he is. I'll reach out and see if I can't get him to perform."

"We need an answer by Wednesday," Kamaya noted. "There are ads that will need to be revised before they go to press. So if you need me to speak with him, I can."

He shook his head. "I can handle it, but if he's not interested I'm not going to push."

"Oh, I'm sure he'll be interested." Bryan grinned.

Wesley shot his friend a look, the gesture flying over Kamaya's head.

"Then I think we're finished here," she said, doing an about-face. She stole a quick glance down at her wristwatch. "I have another meeting to get to. Paxton, if you'll please get any paperwork Wesley has for us, I'd appreciate it. I'd like to review those numbers he put together."

Paxton dropped a tentative hand against her forearm. His voice dropped to a low whisper. "Do you have time for us to talk?"

Kamaya stepped out of his reach, pulling her arm from his grasp. "Maybe later," she said. There was no missing the friction that shifted between them. Wesley eyed them both curiously, not missing the annoyance that had furrowed Kamaya's brow.

She turned and extended her hand to shake his. "Congratulations, Wesley! You've done a great job," she said as her palm glided like silk against his.

There was just a split second of something that Wesley was sure neither of them could explain or define. It passed like a strike of lightning between them. It was a wealth of heat and emotion that startled them both. She snatched her hand from his as he clutched his into a tight fist.

He smiled, the bend of his lush lips showcasing picture-perfect teeth. "Thank you."

Kamaya smiled back. "How do you feel about being the public face of The Wet Bar?"

Wesley's eyes widened. "Excuse me?"

"Our executive board would like to personalize the image somewhat, and we believe that your enthusiasm about the business and your knowledge about the industry make you a good fit. Obviously we would compensate you accordingly, but it would mean that most marketing queries would roll through your office. Obviously The Michelle Initiative would support you as needed, but we're willing to let this be your baby, if you agree."

His gaze narrowed slightly. "Why?"

"This is a very public foray into the adult entertainment business. For personal reasons, the owners would like to distance themselves somewhat. This would allow them that."

"I'd like to think about it and get back to you, if that's okay?"

She nodded. "That's not a problem at all. And if it will help in your decision, know that the compensation would be quite handsome."

Paxton interjected. "For obvious reasons we would need to know *before* the opening."

Wesley nodded. "I understand."

Kamaya took a deep breath. "Paxton will give you all the details about the interview and the film crew that will be here next week, but if you have any other questions or concerns, please give me a call," she said, as she flipped a business card through her fingers and slid it across his palm.

"Thank you. I appreciate that."

And with that, Kamaya turned, almost racing from the room.

"Wow!" Bryan exclaimed. "Damn! That woman is gorgeous! Did you see those hips and whips?" he asked, gesturing with both hands across his chest and then his butt.

Paxton gave him a look, something protective seeming to sweep over his broad shoulders. "She's out of your league. Besides, she's taken."

Bryan shrugged. "The good ones always are."

Wesley bit down on his bottom lip, his best friend's words echoing in his head. *The good ones always are!*

"Sounds like you're going to be coming out of retirement," Bryan teased, when the two men were finally alone. Paxton was long gone after detailing the rest of the business they needed to address, and Bryan and Wesley were now winding down for the night.

Wesley lifted his eyes to stare at his friend. "Excuse you?"

"You know exactly what I'm talking about, *Deuce*!"

Wesley shook his head, a slight smirk pulling at his mouth. "That is not going to happen."

"It will if Miss Boudreaux has something to say about it."

"Well, she doesn't."

"And what if she asks to speak with him herself?"

"Then I'm giving her your telephone number, and you're going to tell her that you're out of the country and a trip back isn't viable."

Bryan laughed. "You expect me to *lie*?"

Wesley laughed. "Damn right!"

"Maybe you should just tell her the truth and let her know you've retired and are out of business."

"I don't make a point of telling anyone about my dancing days. How long has it been now? Hell, I don't even know if I *can* dance anymore! I'm still trying to figure out how she got my stage name."

"Clearly, the woman did her research. You know better than most that we are a small community nationwide. Ask the right woman and she can tell you who the top dancers are at Chocolate City in Atlanta, Chippendales in Vegas, Thunder Down Under, and Black Diamond in New York. And by next month, they'll add their favorites from The Wet Bar to the list."

"But I haven't danced in years!"

"You were one of the best in the business. I learned my best moves from you. Hell, the best of the best learned their moves from you! Your reputation is legendary. Ask any of the guys about Deuce and they will tell you how they aspire to your notoriety."

Wesley sat back in his seat, his hands folded together as if he were in prayer. His mind wandered as he thought about what his friend had said about his former career and his reputation in the industry.

It used to be a running joke that they called him Deuce because of what was in his pants. He was well endowed, and there had been women who'd mused he was packing at least two good feet of solid meat between his thighs. Of course, two feet was a good foot and an inch on the side of ridiculous, but he had run with it and it had paid off. On a good night Wesley had easily pulled over a thousand dollars in tips. A bad night netted him four or five hundred dollars. Had he been able, he would have danced seven nights a week. But since he couldn't, he'd danced Thursday, Friday and Saturday, and for more private parties than he could count. He'd shaken his goods at brides celebrating their last hurrah, divorcees getting their feet re-wet and women who simply enjoyed a good time.

He had purposely avoided the more salacious aspects of the business. He had never had sex with a client or with anyone when he was working. He'd maintained a

certain etiquette when performing, never, ever expos-
ing his bare package. Over the years he had seen some
things from other dancers that made his head spin and
that wasn't how he had wanted to be remembered.

But dancing had served him well. It put him through
school, bought and paid for his first home and had en-
abled him to buy the business he was now building.
He had few regrets and much appreciation for how the
business had treated him. But he wasn't interested in
making a comeback. The past was best left in the past.
He blew hot air past his lips, the weight of the situation
bearing down on his spirit.

He suddenly thought about Kamaya Boudreaux. The
woman had excited him. He had done a good job of con-
taining his interest, and even in those few moments that
had gotten tense between them, he had still found her
thoroughly engaging. But he recognized that she could
be a force to be reckoned with and he instinctively knew
that telling her no wouldn't be as easy as he hoped. Yet
he had every intention of telling the woman no. The
dancer known as Deuce would not be making an appearance at the grand opening of The Wet Bar.

Chapter 4

When Kamaya googled Wesley Walters, 442,000 search results came up. There were twenty-five LinkedIn profiles and just as many Facebook pages. After eliminating an author, an artist, a doctor, a real estate agent and a host of personalities with the name Wesley Walters, she still hadn't found the good-looking black man who'd piqued her curiosity. She blew a soft sigh as she settled back in her upholstered chair.

It had been a good long while since any man had captured her interest the way Wesley Walters had. And because he had her attention, she found herself wanting to vet him as completely as possible. She trusted his association with Paxton because she trusted her friend, but she instinctively knew there was more to the man than even Paxton knew.

As she powered down her computer there was a

knock on her office door. She looked up just as Paxton pushed the entrance open and poked his head in. "Can we talk now?" he asked, eyeing her with an air of indignation.

She returned his look with a raised eyebrow. "Do I detect a hint of attitude?"

Paxton moved into the room, closing the door behind him. He dropped down into the empty seat in front of her desk. "No, you detect a boatload of attitude. What's your problem?"

She crossed her arms over her chest. "My problem?"

"Yeah! You've been giving me the cold shoulder since I told you about me and Laney. What kind of shit is that? You're supposed to be my friend. My best friend!" He tossed up his hands in frustration.

Kamaya shook her head. "You really have some nerve. You tell me you're marrying that wildebeest and I'm suddenly supposed to change how I feel about her? Not saying anything is the best thing I could have done for you and our friendship."

"Wildebeest? Really?"

"Really. Did you forget about her husband? Or does the fact that she has one not matter to you?"

"You know that's only a technicality. She loves me."

"She loves playing you and you enjoy letting her."

"That's low. Now you're sounding like you're bitter. And jealous!"

Kamaya blew a soft sigh. "Paxton, you and I go way back. And because we have a lot of history I'm going to pretend you didn't just say that." She shifted forward in her seat. "Laney is a witch. You know she's a witch. Because I'm your best friend I can tell you she's a witch. Now, if that moose ever does get her divorce, you can marry her if you want to, but I'm not going to lie to you about how I feel about it. When it blows up, I'll be right here to help you pick up the pieces. And then I'm going to tell you I told you so. You're making a mistake. A big one."

"You are so cold!"

"I'm honest. I will always keep it one hundred with you."

He shook his head. "You know you're breaking my heart right now, right?"

"You should have let me have some time, but no, you had to push."

"That's what I do."

"Then you shouldn't get mad when I push back."

He paused for a moment. "So, now what?

"Now nothing. When and if you actually marry that barracuda, I will be there as your friend. I'll be your best man or best woman or whatever, throw you a banging bachelor party and then I'll try to talk you out of it because that's what a true friend would do!"

"Well, can you do one more thing for me?"

"What's that?"

"Can you stop calling my girl names? Please? To hear you tell it she's the star of her own animal kingdom!"

Kamaya shrugged. "Well, if the hoofs fit…"

Paxton rolled his eyes. "Really, Kamaya?"

"Tch!" She sucked her teeth, annoyance wafting over her expression. "Whatever. I promise I'll try. Just keep her away from me until I stop feeling some kind of way."

"I still think it's jealousy. You were really hoping the two of us were going to hook up, weren't you?"

Kamaya narrowed the gaze she leveled in his direction. "Now I know you fell down and bumped your damn head!"

Paxton laughed. "You better be glad I still love you."

"I love you, too!" She changed the subject. "So, tell me more about your friend Wesley."

His eyes widened. "Wesley? What do you want to know?"

"What can you tell me?"

"He's one of the good guys. He was at the top of our class in school. From a middle class working family. Put himself through school working fast food and blue collar jobs. Two and three at a time if I remember correctly. Personally, I always thought he was kind of country but it looks like he's coming up in the world. I like him. I like him a lot. He's not afraid to take risks even if they're safe risks and I've always found him to be honest to a fault. No man should be that honest!"

"That's it?"

"You need more?

She shrugged. "Is he married?"

"I don't think so."

"Gay?"

"That, I'm not sure about. Why? You interested?"

"I like to know who I'm doing business with. Vetting people is a necessary vice when you don't want folks to know your business."

"Which is why you need to come clean and stop pretending you're selling cupcakes for a living. You're no girl scout and they don't give out honor badges in our field of work."

"You handle your business your way. I'll handle my business my way."

"His friend Bryan was gushing over you."

"What did he say?"

"What they all say about your *assets*."

"And what did you say?"

"What I always say. I told him you were already in a relationship."

Kamaya's eyes widened. "Why would you do that? What if Wesley thinks that I really am?"

Paxton chuckled. Before he could give her a retort his cell phone rang, the device chiming from the inner pocket of his jacket. Kamaya watched as he pulled it from the compartment, his eyes lighting up as he answered the call.

"Hey, baby!"

She shook her head as she listened to his side of the conversation.

"No, sweetheart...I...It's not like that...Of course, I love you...I'm on my way, I promise...Laney, don't be...Please, darling..."

Kamaya rolled her eyes.

Paxton suddenly disconnected the call. "I need to cut this gab fest short."

"Awww! Is Laney not happy?" she said, her tone sarcastic. "Does darling need her boo-boo bear?"

"You are mean! I bet when you were a kid you used to kick dogs, torture cats and bully the other girls."

"You're a fool." She blew a heavy sigh. "I think I'm going to take the day tomorrow. Maybe work from home. I need to catch up on some things."

Paxton nodded. "Just touch base with me when you can."

Kamaya nodded. "I will," she said, her gaze narrowing as his cell phone chimed once again.

He took a deep breath as he stole a quick glance

down at the screen. "I'll talk to you later," he said, as he turned abruptly and rushed from the room.

As the door slammed behind him Kamaya sneered, her expression pained. Her best friend's relationship with that woman was proving to be a continuous thorn in both their asses. It made no sense to her why he couldn't see it. She was still shaking her head when she reached for her phone and scrolled through her contacts.

Seconds later, her sister answered the phone.

"Hey, Kamaya, what's up?" Maitlyn answered.

"Are you busy?"

"I was just rocking Zayn to sleep."

"I can call you back."

"No, it's no problem. Zakaria is reading Rose-Lynn her bedtime story and Zayn's already dozed off. I just like to cuddle him as much as I can. When Zakar gets here, Zayn's going to have to share mommy's lap, so I want him to get all the *me* time he can while he's still the little baby."

"You're naming the new baby Zakar! I like that!"

"It was Zakaria's idea. You know how he is about his sons! I was leaning toward Aloysius."

Kamaya laughed. "Aloysius Sayed? Really!"

"It has a ring to it."

"If you want your son to grow up with psychological issues."

Maitlyn laughed with her. "My baby would be just fine."

"Zakar Sayed has a jazzier ring to it. Zak is right on this one."

"I hate to admit it, but I know! Just don't tell him I said that!"

Kamaya smiled. She instinctively knew her sister

was leaning to kiss her son's forehead, nuzzling her cheek against his little face. "You sound happy, Maitlyn."

"I am. Though, I'll be ecstatic in about six weeks when this baby comes. But that's not what you called me for. What's up?"

"I need Zak to run a background check on someone for me."

"Ooh! This sounds serious. Who is he?"

"His name is Wesley Walters and he's someone I just need to know more about."

"So you're running background checks on random men now?"

"There is absolutely nothing *random* about *this* man!"

"That sounds even more intriguing! Are you two dating?"

"We just met. We might be doing some business together and I just want to make sure he's on the up and up."

"So this is just a professional query?"

Kamaya shook her head, imagining the smug expression on her sister's face. "Just find out *everything* that you can about him. Please. Professional *and* personal."

Maitlyn laughed. "Send me what you have on him and I'll see what Zakaria can do. Did you think about calling Mason or Kendrick? You know they both would have checked him out for you."

"I'd like to keep the brother brigade out of my business, if I can. You know how that is."

"I do! I'll take care of it, sister dear!"

"Thank you."

"You're very welcome! Now I need you to do me a favor."

"Should I be scared?"

Maitlyn laughed again. "Call your mother and give her something. Anything! Just make sure it tides her over so she stops asking all of us what's going on with you. Tell her you're dating the entire Saints roster or that you just broke up with a drug dealer or that you have a new boyfriend who lives in Katmandu. Just tell her something. Please!"

The two women laughed heartily together.

"I swear this entire family is crazy!" Kamaya finally muttered as she gasped for breath, tears of amusement streaming down her face.

Agreement shimmered in Maitlyn's tone. "Yeah, we are!"

Kamaya Boudreaux was the sister of Mason Boudreaux, III. Making the connection suddenly had Wesley in his feelings. He had idolized the billionaire since attending a seminar where the high-profile executive had spoken. It had been shortly after the sale of Boudreaux's hotel-owning company to Stallion Enterprises, an even bigger conglomerate in Dallas, Texas. Mason Boudreaux had owned, managed, leased and franchised, through various subsidiaries, over four thousand hotels and more than six hundred and fifty thousand guest rooms in one hundred countries and territories around the world. Selling Boudreaux International Hotels and Resorts when he was just thirty-seven was a testament to his hard work and dedication. He had been an inspiration, and Wesley had been a fan ever since.

At that conference, one of many Wesley regularly

attended to boost his knowledge, Mason had talked for
over an hour about how he'd achieved professional success to the detriment of his personal life. But he had said
that a shift in priorities and a good woman were making
the next stage of his career even more profitable than
the first. He had spoken about the importance of balance, focus and commitment in doing what you loved,
where a dream job was so much more than a monthly
paycheck. And he'd shared how the emotional support
of family and friends made it all worthwhile.

Now Wesley had discovered that the woman he was
now in business with was related to the man he'd idolized since forever. He was kicking himself for not having made the connection sooner. He closed the cover
on his iPad and the article he'd just finished reading
about the newest Boudreaux venture. Mason's new company, Boudreaux Forensics, analyzed corporate investments to quantify portfolio losses and provide opinions
regarding investment suitability. Mason was helping
companies grow like he had grown his own. The interview had been two pages long and had included a brief
paragraph on his personal life. There had been a family photograph, and as Wesley had scanned the image,
seeing Kamaya's stern expression as she stood between
her brothers had caught him completely off guard. He
blew a deep sigh.

He reached across the desk for the contract and documents that Paxton had left with him. Essentially, The
Michelle Initiative was distancing itself from The Wet
Bar franchises. Their agreement gave him a controlling
interest in the company's development, first right of re-
fusal for all future franchise properties and allowed him
a level of interest in the business that any entrepreneur

would have been excited about. The agreement also made him a contracted consultant to the parent company and had him reporting directly to Kamaya Boudreaux. That factor was particularly intriguing to him.

Researching the parent company hadn't turned up anything that had him overly concerned. It was a consortium of family-friendly businesses, so he understood their reluctance to expose their involvement with and expansion into the adult entertainment industry. Since it was privately owned, outsiders learned only what the company wanted them to know, and he liked the prospect of being allowed into the inner sanctum. He found it hard to believe that Kamaya wouldn't be taking business advice from her brother. Wesley longed to meet the executive and possibly learn from them both. And if he were honest, he was excited about the prospect of working closely with Kamaya. *Very excited.*

He dropped the folder of contracts into his briefcase. His attorney had already assured him that he was gaining more than he was risking. They had been overly generous. But despite feeling like he'd won the biggest prize at the state fair, something still didn't feel right. He had questions and he wanted the answers from Kamaya Boudreaux. And he wasn't going to sign until he got them.

Kamaya had cleaned her house from top to bottom. She'd dusted cobwebs out of the ceiling's corners, washed windows, polished all of the wood furniture, bleached the bathroom tile, watered the plants and tossed some vegetables and frozen chicken into her brand-new Crock-Pot. If anyone had asked, she wouldn't have been able to tell them what had triggered that maternal instinct to suddenly nest, but when she'd opened her eyes that morning the need had been almost desperate. She'd risen intending to clean until the home was spotless, and with one last swipe across the marble counters in her kitchen, it finally was.

After giving the timer on her Crock-Pot one last check, she moved toward her bedroom to shower. She'd just stripped out of her clothes and was heading for the master bathroom when her cell phone rang, the number on the screen was not one she recognized. Despite the initial instinct to ignore it, curiosity got the best of her.

"Hello?"

"May I speak to Kamaya Boudreaux, please?"

She hesitated, the familiar voice making her stomach do a twirl and a flip. The thick Southern drawl was unmistakable, Wesley Walters's deep baritone voice sounded rich and thick and decadently sweet. Kamaya felt her whole body begin to quiver with excitement. "Wesley Walters, hello! This is a surprise," she said, as she felt her face pull into a full grin.

"I hope I'm not disturbing you."

"Not at all. What can I do for you?"

"I was reviewing the contracts Paxton left and I had some questions. I was hoping you'd be able to meet me for a cup of coffee to discuss them."

"Now?"

"If you're not busy."

Kamaya paused, dropping down onto the side of her freshly made bed. "So, what kind of questions do you have?"

"Nothing major. Just some things that I need clarification on."

"Paxton couldn't help you?"

"There's no point in wasting my time with the middleman. Why ask for a yes from the man who can only say no?"

Kamaya chuckled. "I'll give you that! I can meet up with you."

"There's a great little coffee shop on Magazine Street between Race and Orange Streets."

"Mojo's. I know it well. It's one of my favorite spots."

"Mine, too. Let's say in about an hour?"

"Make it two."

"I'll see you there in two hours," he said, then he disconnected the call.

Kamaya took a deep breath and then a second to calm the quiver of nerves that had consumed her. She pressed her knees tightly together, stalling the slight rumble that prickled her sweet spot. She couldn't begin to understand why her body had her feeling like an adolescent with a first crush. "Get a hold of yourself!" she muttered under her breath.

She glanced to the clock on her nightstand. The coffee shop was some twenty minutes away from her front door. She had more than enough time to soak in a hot tub, primp and get there with time to spare. She was still holding on to her cell phone when it vibrated in her palm, surprising her. When she answered, her sister's voice boomed in greeting on the other end.

"Hey, Maitlyn!" she responded.

"So, tell me about this man again?"

"What man?"

"Don't play. You know what man."

"Why? What did you find out?"

"Walter Wesley has quite a reputation."

"What do you mean?

"Where do I start? For one, he's got an estimated net worth of…"

Kamaya interrupted. "I know his financials. I've been reviewing his banking numbers for weeks now. I wanted to know if he's married!"

Maitlyn laughed. "No. He's single. No children. He's not currently involved in a romantic relationship, but he's got quite a fan club of female followers."

"What do you mean?"

"I sent you the link. It's an old Myspace page that was practically archived. It hasn't had any activity in some time, but it's definitely about him."

Kamaya moved to the laptop on her desk, pulling up her sister's email message. "What kind of fan page is it?"

"Something one of his admirers put together on his behalf, but it looks like he interacted regularly to keep the ladies updated on his whereabouts."

"I don't understand."

Maitlyn laughed. "Your friend use to be an exotic dancer. A very popular one."

There was a moment of stunned silence as Kamaya processed the information. It had been the last thing she'd expected her sister to discover about the man.

The amusement in Maitlyn's tone shifted to something more serious. "Is this anything I need to be concerned about, Kamaya?"

Kamaya blew a soft sigh. "He and I are meeting in an hour for coffee to discuss some concerns he has with his contracts."

"Seems like a good time to discuss the concerns you might have about his employment choices," Maitlyn countered.

Kamaya rolled her eyes, her sister's comment irritating her for reasons she couldn't comprehend. "Is there anything else?" she questioned.

"No. On paper he seems like a really great guy. He has fared well in business, so a professional partnership would probably serve you well. Anything else you'll have to figure out on your own, kiddo!"

"Thanks for the help."

"You're very welcome. By the way, you never told me about this business venture you two are considering doing together."

Kamaya laughed. "It's just an amusement park kind of thing. Something I'll probably pass on."

Maitlyn chuckled. "Okay. It's your lie. Tell it any way you want to!"

For a good ten minutes Kamaya sat pouring through the information on the Myspace page that her sister had linked her to. There were multiple photos and a ton of comments from fans. Reading through them was entertaining. She actually lost count of the women who'd posted their telephone numbers, hoping that the dancer named Deuce would reach out and touch them.

There was one link to a video. It was old and slightly grainy but it was definitely Wesley Walters in all his glory. He wore skin and a cock sheath, the G-string with an oversized length of fabric stretching over the package between his legs. He'd been exceptionally blessed, and she imagined that when he'd been born and the angels were doling out body parts, he'd gotten his and then some.

He had exceptional rhythm and moved with a sensual ease. His gyrations were downright nasty in the most tasteful way. Everything about him and how he moved was a contradiction, and the women were wild for him. Kamaya watched the three-minute clip a few times before finally closing the link and shutting down her computer. She blew warm breath, the room feeling like someone had turned up the heat, and she was close to combusting. She swore, profanity flooding the room. She needed to get ready. But her warm bath would have to turn into a very cold shower, instead.

Chapter 5

She'd worn low-slung boyfriend jeans with a white button-up blouse and strappy gold sandals with a stiletto heel. Her hair was pulled back into a messy bun and gold hoop earrings adorned her earlobes. As she stepped into the room, heads turned, observers eyeing her appreciatively, one male too many smiling as she eased past.

Wesley sat forward and upright in his seat at the sight of her. His heartbeat suddenly felt like a drum line gone rampant, the beautiful woman taking his breath away. As she made her way to his table he stood up, greeting her with an eager expression and bright smile.

"Kamaya, hello!" He extended his hand to shake hers.

"Hi!" she said, her smile pulling wide and full across her face. "It's good to see you again." She snatched her fingers from his, a wave of intense heat searing their touch. She drew her fingers into a tight fist, dropping her arm to her side as she gently clutched the side of her pants leg.

"I appreciate you taking time out to meet with me." He pulled out a chair and gestured for her to take a seat beside him.

Kamaya dropped into the wooden chair gratefully, as her knees were shaking, threatening to send her to the floor. She took a deep breath and held it briefly.

"What can I get you?" he asked as he gestured toward the counter and the line forming for orders.

She glanced at the menu and the specialty drinks noted on the blackboard. "I think I'll try an Almond Joy cappuccino, thank you."

With a quick nod he moved toward the counter, striding like a man on a mission. Kamaya tried not to stare. At least, not so obviously that he would notice. But staring seemed almost mandatory.

Wesley was one good-looking man. He wore a form-fitting, black cotton T-shirt that flattered his exceptionally broad chest, and his shoulders and biceps bulged from regular workouts in a gym. He filled the black denim jeans he wore nicely. The distinctive stitching on the back pockets of his Levi's curved sweetly around his backside. The bubble of his ass was so large and high that she imagined she could rest a glass on the ledge and not have it fall off. She herself had a great backside, but his was even bigger and better. She couldn't help but imagine herself squeezing each cheek in the palms of her hands, fueling a fantasy that suddenly had her panting ever so slightly. Black Timberlands completed his ensemble.

She shifted forward in her seat, her hands folded in her lap as he returned to her side. He carried a tray with two ceramic mugs of coffee laden with cream and oversized slices of buttery lemon pie.

"This is one of their best desserts," he said, as he sat back down in his chair. "I thought you might like to give it a try. Or, if you prefer, I could get you coffee cake?"

"The pie is fine. It looks really good," she said, as she accepted the dessert he set gently on the table in front of her.

She took a sip of her coffee, pausing briefly as he shut his eyes and whispered a quick blessing over his food. The gesture was slightly unnerving, and Kamaya was mildly embarrassed that she'd not thought to do the same.

Her mother had often admonished her to do better, and for the first time Kamaya actually wished she had. She couldn't help but wonder if Wesley had noticed and what it had him thinking about her. She took a deep breath, and then a second, to stall the quiver of anxiety that had quickly taken hold.

She suddenly realized he was staring at her. She lifted her eyes to his, their gazes locking. The moment was surreal, seeming like a dream gone awry. But there was still something comfortable about the look the handsome man was giving her. She felt the corners of her mouth lift in an easy smile. Wesley smiled back, and in that brief moment she realized he'd been as nervous as she was.

He seemed to read her mind. "I apologize. I'm not usually so…awkward."

She nodded. "I hope it's not something I did."

He shook his head. "Not at all. I…well… I just want to make a good impression, I think."

Kamaya nodded. There was something refreshing about his openness. She had wanted to do the same thing but she was hardly about to be as honest about it. She shifted to neutral ground. Business, her comfort zone. "So, tell me about these concerns and questions you have that were so important."

Wesley took a deep breath. He'd been practicing how he planned to say what was on his mind since getting up the nerve to call her. In all honesty, he hadn't expected her to answer the phone and when she had there had been no turning back.

His large hands were wrapped around his mug. He finally released the air he'd been holding deep in his lungs. "I'm a man who likes to know who I'm doing business with. I think you of all people can understand why I would want to tread cautiously"

"I do."

"Well, I've done some research. To be honest, I wanted to trace the ownership of the business. To see who it was I was getting in bed with, so to speak."

Kamaya felt herself tense slightly. Her eyes widened. She realized he'd shaken a hornet's nest, not at all prepared for her sting. She was even more intrigued now, his boldness impressing her. She shifted in her chair. "And what did you discover?" she asked, expending some effort to maintain a casual tone to her voice.

"I kept running into one dead end after another. But what I did learn was quite intriguing. Now I have more questions than I have answers."

Kamaya nodded. A pregnant pause grew thick and full between them as she pondered his comment. She took a slow sip of her coffee before resting her cup back against the tabletop. He was still eyeing her intently. "I'm sure you can appreciate the owner's need for privacy," she said.

"I can appreciate that *you* would like to keep what *you* do secret, but if I'm going to partner with you I'd appreciate knowing why."

Kamaya bristled. "Excuse me?

"It just made sense. Your interest in the company's operations feels very personal. Someone has gone to great lengths to conceal the company structure and it took some serious digging to tie the adult operations of the company back to the parent organization. Again, I had to ask myself why someone would go to the trouble. But when I researched your family ties, well, like I said, it just made sense. So, why did you?"

Wesley had rested his elbows against the table, dropping his chin atop his clasped hands. Kamaya had never before imagined anyone being curious enough about The Michelle Initiative to do what he had done. She'd never intended to take her company public, so only two other people besides Paxton had needed to know her connection to each individual company under the business umbrella, and she paid both her attorney and her accountant handsomely to keep that information secret.

She had often wondered how she might respond if the question was posed, but as Wesley sat waiting for her to reply, none of the responses she'd imagined came to her. She took a bite of her pie, needing a moment to reflect. She finally spoke. "The pie is good. Great choice."

Wesley laughed. The tone was creamy and thick and slightly intoxicating. He sat back in his chair, his body relaxing as he continued to eye her curiously.

She took a deep breath. "But we're not partners. And the legal agreement that we're about to enter into doesn't necessitate you knowing anything I don't want you to know."

"No, technically we aren't partners. But I believe for the business to grow where I think we'd both like to see it, it's going to require a mutual respect and equal effort from both of us. And that starts with honesty." He grinned from ear to ear, and his eyes narrowed slightly. "But I think you want to tell me. There's something in your expression that tells me you're ready to open up and have someone other than our friend Paxton know what's in your heart."

She chuckled softly. "So now you're a mind reader?"

"Of sorts. I didn't get this far without being able to read people."

"People? Or women? Because I'd venture to guess that you have a few secrets of your own. Are you willing to share?"

There was a glint of something mischievous in his gaze, the look he gave her slightly smug. "So is this an impasse? The I'll show you mine if you show me yours moment?"

Kamaya laughed, the low trill causing a rumble of heat to simmer through his lower quadrant. She leaned forward, the gesture almost conspiratorial as she motioned for him to meet her halfway. "Showing you mine isn't the problem," she said, her seductive tone teasing.

Her tongue peeked past the line of her lush lips, and for a split second Wesley felt his breath catch deep in his chest. Her comment actually surprised him and he felt a blush of heat warm his cheeks. He laughed again as they both eased backward in their chairs.

Kamaya shook her head. She took a deep breath, and her gaze met his evenly.

As she blew warm breath past her lips, Wesley found himself wondering what it might be like to kiss the sugar from her mouth. Imagining what she might feel like in his arms suddenly had him heated. He shook the sensation away, twisting about in his seat as she continued to speak.

"Since you've done your research then I'm sure you know of my brother Mason's business accomplishments."

"I do. I heard him speak at a business seminar a few years ago. I have great respect for his past and current endeavors."

"And I'm sure you also know that my parents are both quite active in the community?"

He nodded.

"My mother works closely with the National Center on Sexual Exploitation. My father served on their board for many years. It's one of their many missions to oppose sexual exploitation of any kind. They rally against pornography, sex trafficking, prostitution, violence and abuse against women and children, and a host of other man-made ills. The adult entertainment aspect of my business would not sit well with them. And yes, it is *my* business."

"So they don't know about your connection to The Michelle Initiative?"

"They know I own the business and its chains of gas stations, groceries and convenience stores. They don't know anything else. And I work very hard to keep it that way."

"And your brother?"

"There has never been any need for him to know. In the beginning he gave me great advice that allowed me to grow the business. When I made the decision to take it in the direction I took it, I kept him out of the loop. He would have told the old people and they would have insisted I stop."

"And you didn't want to stop?"

"When you consider that the sex industry is a fifty-seven *billion*-dollar business annually, why would I?"

"So, are you thinking of doing more than strip clubs? I know you have sex toys and the sex health division. Are you considering pornography or...?"

She shook her head vehemently. "Not at all. I'm only planning to go but so far. And my strip clubs will never feature women. We have more than enough of that. But when you consider that here in the United States there are more strip clubs than any other nation in the world, employing hundreds of thousands of people, why not claim a small piece of that pie? Statistics show that a single gentlemen's club in a major metropolitan area can average up to twenty million dollars per year in gross revenues. *Male* strip clubs are truly an untapped revenue stream and I plan to corner the market. If I don't, someone else will. So why not me?"

Wesley nodded. "I like how you think. I look forward to sharing a piece of *that* pie with you!"

Kamaya grinned. She pushed her empty plate away from her. "So, what else did you find out about me?" she asked.

Wesley shrugged his wide shoulders toward the ceiling. "You like country music. You eat way too much fast food and you're vicious when guys show you any interest."

Kamaya smiled. "Facebook is not an appropriate spot to do research on me. It is, however, an ideal place to throw folks off when they're trying to be nosy. You should have done what I did and hired a private investigator."

The faintest shimmer of surprise crossed Wesley's expression. "A private investigator? You went through a lot of trouble."

"You don't really think I would go into business with just anyone, do you?"

"You could have just asked. I don't have anything to hide. I'm an open book."

"I'm sure that's not true," Kamaya said, chuckling softly.

"You'll never know, will you? I'm sure there's nothing else I can tell you about myself that you don't already know."

"Oh, there's something!"

"What's that?"

"Will you be dancing on opening night, Deuce?"

Wesley laughed heartily, thoroughly amused by Kamaya. Calling him out on his own secret had given her much pleasure, and he had to admit he found her resourcefulness sexy as hell.

"How did your private investigator find out that I was Deuce?"

"She's very good at what she does. Having a husband and a brother who both work for the Secret Service didn't hurt, either."

"She?"

"My sister Maitlyn. If it exists, she can find it."

"Wow! So you do like to keep things in the family."

"Some things." She smiled sweetly. "So, tell me about this second career of yours."

He shrugged his broad shoulders. "It was a means to an end," he said, explaining the hows and whys of his choices.

When he was done, Kamaya was still staring at him intently. Her expression was a mix of amusement and reflection, clearly taking it all in, contemplating it and forming an opinion about him and all that he was.

"I'm impressed," she said finally.

"Thank you. And, much like you, my parents wouldn't necessarily approve so I've never told them."

"So you do get it?"

"I do. With my mother, if it's not ordained by God himself, it can't be any good. And my father literally put the *old* in old school!"

Kamaya laughed. "Do you have any siblings?"

"An older sister. Lillian is a doctor. Right now she's doing missionary work in Gambia. She definitely wouldn't understand or be supportive. She wanted me to go to medical school and follow in her footsteps."

"If it really came down to it, I could probably tell my sister Maitlyn, but then it would put her in the position to lie to everyone else and I can't do that to her."

Wesley leaned forward in his seat. "So what about your boyfriend? How does he feel about your line of adult businesses?"

"What boyfriend?"

"Your girlfriend?"

Kamaya laughed. "Neither. I think you've received some inaccurate information!"

"Paxton had said you were involved with someone. I just assumed…"

"Fatal mistake. You should know better. To be successful you need to deal only in facts, *not* assumptions. Business 101!"

He tilted his head at her. "Touché!"

"I'm not in a relationship. I don't have a significant other. And it's a point of consternation for my family. My mother in particular. I'm the last of the brood who doesn't have a spouse or children. She thinks there's something wrong with me."

Wesley nodded. "So far I've been lucky. Mom and Dad know I'm about building my career right now. I'm sure in a few more years I'll be hearing it, too, the family wondering what's going on!"

"Things could change in a few years. You never know."

Wesley met her deep stare with one of his own. "You're right. You never know."

"You still didn't answer my question, though. Can we count on you to dance for us opening night, Deuce?"

He shook his head. "Deuce doesn't exist anymore. So, no, I don't think he'll be making any appearances any time soon."

"Not even if it'll be good for this business we're growing together?"

He gave her a look, his eyes wide. "Trust me when I tell you, I really wasn't that good."

Kamaya laughed. "That's a lie. I saw the video!"

Her amusement was infectious and Wesley laughed with her, the beauty of the moment resonating between them.

Wesley reached into the briefcase that rested beside his chair leg. He passed her the folder of documents. "They're all signed," he said, as he extended his hand to shake hers. "I look forward to working with you, Kamaya Boudreaux."

She slid her palm against his, the warmth of his touch heating her spirit. "Same here, Wesley Walters. I imagine we're going to make a formidable team."

"Team! I like that."

"You should. Because it's so out of character for me! I don't usually play well with others."

He chuckled. "Then I'm glad you chose me to play with first."

A cup of coffee and a few questions kept Kamaya and Wesley talking for almost three hours. After sharing more than either had planned, they stood, saying their goodbyes and making plans to see each other again.

"I would really love to take you to dinner," Wesley said, as he walked Kamaya to her car.

"Are you asking me out on a date, Wesley Walters?"

He grinned. "I am. With one condition."

"What's that?"

"We don't talk business. I get the impression that's not an easy thing for you to do. So will you accept the challenge?"

As they reached her car, she smiled as she nodded her head. "I'd love to."

"I mean it about not talking business."

Kamaya laughed. "Boy, please! You really don't know me."

He laughed with her. "I don't, but I definitely look forward to changing that."

Wesley opened the door of her vehicle. The air between them was thick and heavy, carnal energy sweeping from one to the other, fervent with desire. It was intense and unexpected, and left them both feeling a little awkward and definitely excited about what might come.

"Drive safely, Kamaya," he whispered softly, watching as she slid into the driver's seat.

She nodded. "You too, Wesley. Have a really good night."

Kamaya was sifting through spreadsheets when the intercom sounded for her attention. She slid one set of financial projections off to the side and reached for another as she ignored the persistent chime. The knock on the office door finally moved her to respond. "Yes!" she snapped, clearly annoyed by the interruption. "I said I didn't want to be interrupted!"

Virginia opened the door and peeked her head in the room. "I'm sorry. I know you didn't want to be disturbed but Wesley Walters is here to see you. He insists he has an appointment but I don't have anything on your calendar. He refuses to leave until he talks to you."

Kamaya's eyes widened in surprise. "Wesley's here? In the office?"

Virginia nodded. "What do you want me to do?"

Kamaya's gaze skated from side to side as she collected her thoughts. He had called her earlier, leaving a message that he was still interested in dinner and imploring her to set a date. She hadn't returned his call, having second thoughts about having dinner with the man.

There was no denying that something was simmering between them. After their shared coffee, leaving him had actually been hard, emotions surfacing that Kamaya wasn't familiar or comfortable with. She couldn't begin to imagine anything good coming from what she found herself feeling and so she was questioning if spending personal time with him would be a good thing for her, or her business. The doubt must have registered across her face.

"Are you okay?" Virginia asked, concern dancing in the woman's ocean blue eyes.

Kamaya took a deep inhale of air as she sat back in her seat. A moment passed before she nodded. "Yes. Send him in," she said finally.

With a tilt of her head the other woman turned on her low heels. A quick minute later she ushered Wesley into the inner sanctum, shot Kamaya one last look and then closed the door leaving them alone.

"Wesley! This is a surprise." Kamaya moved onto her feet and rounded the desk toward him. Her hand extended in greeting.

"I hope I'm not interrupting," Wesley said as he moved closer. He came to an abrupt stop when the subtle fragrance of her perfume wafted into his personal space. They shook hands, the polite touch inciting a current of electricity between them. He gasped, a slight smile pulling at his mouth.

Kamaya took in another breath of air as she gestured toward the leather sofa that decorated the space. "Not at all. Please have a seat. What brings you here?" She dropped down onto the cushioned bench beside him.

"I could say I was in the neighborhood but that would be a lie." He smiled, the warmth of it filling his face. "I wanted to see you. And I was hoping to pin down that date for dinner."

Kamaya's gaze skated over his face, noting the sweet bend of his mouth and the way his brow furrowed slightly. There was something hopeful in his gaze as he eyed her. She took another deep breath to stall the quiver of energy that pulsed deep in the pit of her stomach.

"About that," she said as she stood abruptly, moving to lean against the edge of her desk. "Do you really think it's a good idea that we see each other socially? I mean…well…"

"You mean you're getting cold feet." He stood and closed the distance between them as he moved to her side.

Their gazes locked as they stood staring at each other. Kamaya felt moisture rising to the surface of her skin, perspiration threatening to dampen places it had no business. She inhaled swiftly, frozen in place as the heat from his body blended nicely with her own.

Kamaya found herself staring at his mouth, imagining the feel of his lips against her skin, his tongue trailing a damp line over her flesh. She suddenly realized she was panting slightly. She turned, her eyes blinking rapidly.

She took a deep breath before she spoke. "Look, it's not about cold feet. I just…well…" There was a moment of pause as she gathered her thoughts, wanting to find just the right words to explain herself.

Wesley was eyeing her intently. He was awed by how beautiful she was. Kamaya was a gorgeous woman without an ounce of effort. She had a natural glow, an intoxicating aura that had him drunk with wanting. He bit down against his bottom lips as he fought the urge to reach a hand out to touch her. Wanting to trace the back of his fingers against her skin. He crossed his arms over his chest and clasped both hands beneath his armpits. He took a step and shifted his weight back, needing to widen the distance between them just slightly.

Kamaya finally spoke, shifting her gaze back to his. "Look, I have to be honest with you."

"I expect nothing less," he interjected, his eyes dancing with hers.

"I don't do relationships and you seem like a relationship kind of guy. I would hate for us to...well...you know." She suddenly stammered, beginning to lose herself in his deep gaze. She blew a gust of air past her lips. "It just wouldn't work and we would still be obligated to work together," she concluded.

"Are you always so negative?"

"Excuse me?"

"You've already broken up with me and we haven't even had our first official date."

"I didn't break up with you!"

"Yes, you did. Which means you know we're going to have a relationship and, because you're not the relationship type, that scares you."

"It doesn't..."

"But that's okay," he said as he took a step toward her, closing that distance he'd needed moments earlier. "I'm not scared and I'm not going away, Kamaya Boudreaux. I am a relationship kind of guy and I believe you and I are going to be magic together." He slid the pad of his index finger across the line of her profile. "So, how does tomorrow work for you and what time should I pick you up?"

A slow smile widened across Kamaya's face. She clasped her hand over his, drawing it back down to his side. A low laugh eased past her lips. "You are so full of yourself," she said, the comment ringing warmly through the air.

He laughed with her. "Yes, I am. It's what you like about me!"

Chapter 6

He couldn't get her out of his mind. It had been three weeks since their coffee date and Wesley hadn't been able to stop thinking about Kamaya. He felt slightly bewitched. And completely out of sorts.

Everything about their encounter had warmed his spirit. She had been funny, her dry sense of humor moving him to laugh more than he had lately. She was smart, her intelligence challenging his own. She gave as good as she got. And she gave often, quick with her quips and smart remarks. It didn't take much for him to realize that holding his own with her would keep him on his toes. A time or two she'd actually had him blushing. Kamaya had no filters, speaking her mind on any and every subject that moved her.

He pulled clothes out of his closet, trying to decide what to wear. After he had stopped by her office unannounced they had made tentative plans. He had called her the very next day to confirm, only to be told something had come up. Since then, they had talked many times, each ending their day in conversation. Kamaya hadn't been overly helpful with the planning of their first get-together, insisting that he surprise her. But he had sensed that she wasn't a woman who actually liked surprises.

What he did know was that there was nothing pretentious about Kamaya Boudreaux. Wining and dining her at some five-star establishment wouldn't impress this woman. He knew enough to know that she'd been to some of the finest restaurants around the world, so what the best of New Orleans had to offer wasn't going to be good enough to make the kind of impression he wanted. He wanted this first time to be one she never forgot. A moment in her history that she would one day regale her grandchildren with stories about. The sound of his cell phone suddenly interrupted his thoughts. For a brief second he feared another cancellation until he looked at the caller ID. He smiled.

"Hello, beautiful lady!"

"Hello, son! How are you?"

"I'm good, ma. How about you?"

"I have no complaints so it's a good day. Do you have a minute?"

"For you, I have as many as you need."

Annie gigged softly. "I want to take your daddy on a cruise for our anniversary. We've never been on a cruise before and you know how that man can be! I could use your help making that happen."

Wesley laughed. "I can do that. Just let me know what you need me to do."

"For starters you can help me convince him the ship won't capsize while he's on it."

"I'll call him."

"Thank you, baby. So what are you up to?"

"I'm going on a date. I was just getting dressed."

"A date? Do I know this young woman? Where did you meet her?"

Wesley dropped down on the corner of his bed, his extended legs crossed at the ankles. "Her name's Kamaya. Kamaya Boudreaux. She and I will be working together on a business project. And ma, she's...well... she's something special!"

"You sound happy, baby!"

"I don't know that I've ever felt this way about any woman. Kamaya challenges me. She's not going to give me an easy time. If I don't come correct she probably won't give me the time of day."

"I'm sure that girl knows the kind of man you are. She should consider herself lucky that you're even interested in her."

"Says the best mother in the whole wide world!"

"I know that's right!" Annie laughed heartily. "And how long have you and this young lady known each other?"

"A few weeks now. We met when she had a business proposal that I was interested in. I invited her out for coffee and we had a really great time. Then I invited her to dinner but with her schedule we've been playing tag trying to make that happen. But we've talked on the phone every day and I've really been enjoying getting to know her."

"Do you know anything about her family?"

"She comes from a very good family. A big family.

Her brother is Mason Boudreaux. I don't know if you remember me talking about him."

"He's that young man who spoke at that seminar you went to a while back. The man you were so excited about meeting."

"That's him."

"Does she go to church?"

"She's very grounded in her faith."

"You should invite her to go to church with you, Wesley. You don't want to be in a relationship with any woman who doesn't keep God in her heart."

He chuckled, having heard his mother's mantras many times before. "I appreciate the advice, ma. I really do."

"Well, just take things slow. You don't need to rush into anything."

"You rushed. You and daddy knew each other for two days when he asked you to marry him and you said yes."

"That's true but I also made him wait a year before the marriage happened. I needed to be sure."

"You were sure after two days."

"I was but your daddy didn't need to know that."

There was a momentary pause before Wesley spoke. "How did you know, ma? How did you know dad was the man you wanted to spend the rest of your life with?"

He could hear his mother taking a deep breath before she answered. "You just know. There's a feeling you get deep in your gut and you trust it with everything in your heart. Just like you knew Brenda-Joy was the wrong woman for you, you'll know when the right woman comes along."

"Thank you. I love you, ma!"

"I love you, too, son. You have yourself a good time and I'll call you tomorrow to check on you."

Minutes later Wesley admired his reflection in the full-length mirror that adorned his closet door. His fresh haircut was pristine and edged to perfection. He'd selected a handcrafted, dark blue, Charles Dean two-piece suit with the signature peak lapel and white dress shirt that opened at the two-button collar. With a quick adjustment of his cuffs he turned and moved through the house toward the kitchen.

An oversized picnic basket sat on the countertop. He'd packed it earlier, and after one last check to insure that he hadn't forgotten anything, he headed out the door.

Kamaya had been trying on clothes for over an hour. She didn't have a clue what she should wear and it was taking more energy than she cared to exert to try and figure it out. She cut an eye at Maitlyn who was laughing at her hysterically.

"Why are you here?" Kamaya asked, her hands clutching both hips.

"Because..." Maitlyn gasped, catching her breath. "Because you're actually going on a real date and someone needed to record it for posterity."

Kamaya blew an exasperated sigh. She was going on a date and she was still in awe of how that had happened. It was as if she had never dated before and this was her very first time. She was actually nervous, and she couldn't begin to explain why.

Wesley had called her the day after they'd met for coffee. It had surprised her and it shouldn't have. She had believed him when he had said he wanted to take her to dinner. But for reasons she couldn't explain she hadn't trusted it. Yet he had called, wanting her to choose a date, a place and time. At best, she'd been dismissive, promising to call him back. Then she hadn't. So he'd come searching her out.

Even after he had shown up at her office she'd had doubts. She had hesitated instead, putting the onus back on him to decide, and now, almost three weeks later here they were, about to spend the afternoon with each other. Three weeks later because she'd cancelled on him six times, until she couldn't think of any more excuses to put him off.

There was something about Wesley Walters that intrigued her and had her wanting to know more about the man. Since their first phone call they'd talked every day. After two weeks of conversation he had begun to start his morning, and hers, in prayer. The first time it had been disconcerting. Then she had come to look forward to his morning ministry, something his mother apparently did with him on a daily basis. His faith was important to him, and his sharing that with her was a reminder that her own was important to her, as well.

Then she had started to call him in the evenings, to see how his day had gone and to wish him a good-night when neither of them could keep their eyes open. They found a routine with each other, and balance, and everything about it felt right to her, and comfortable.

And now that they were actually going to be in each other's company for an extended period of time, she was actually nervous. Because she didn't do relationships. She did one-night stands and casual acquaintances. Men had been like her line of sex toys, useful when necessary and expendable when not. But Wesley and what was growing between them was different.

"Will you please help me get dressed? I don't know what to wear."

"Usually you'd throw on a pair of jeans and a T-shirt. Why is this day any different?"

"Because…well…because I want to look nice," she replied, throwing yet another dress onto the floor.

Maitlyn had been lying across Kamaya's bed. She suddenly sat upright, her eyes widening. "You really like this guy!"

Kamaya cut a nervous eye in her direction. "I just want to look nice, Maitlyn. Don't read anything else into it, please."

Her sister laughed. "Miss In Control is suddenly feeling a little offsides. I'm reading a lot into that!"

Kamaya rolled her eyes. "I hate you! Help me find something to wear! Please!"

Maitlyn grinned. "Well, for starters, stop trying on all those dresses. Did you buy any of them?"

"No. *Your* mother did. She was trying to spruce up my wardrobe."

"That explains it."

"Explains what?"

"Why each of them make you look like an old church mother."

"They're not *that* bad."

"They really are." Maitlyn rose from the bed, moving into Kamaya's walk-in closet. "Where is he taking you for lunch?"

"I don't know. I told him I didn't want to overdress, so whatever he chooses to do should just be casual so I can dress comfortably. He agreed, except he asked that

I not wear sweats or jeans." Kamaya blew a soft sigh. "Maybe I should just call and cancel."

"You are not canceling," Maitlyn said. She began to flip through the clothes racks, shifting garments from one end to the other. "Now that's more like it!" she exclaimed, holding up a tailored jumpsuit. The price tags were still attached to the sleeve. "This is so you and it's cute!"

"I didn't buy that, either. I think it's Tarah's, to be honest with you. Mom brought it over when she was cleaning out our room."

"Well, it's perfect. Put it on." Maitlyn passed the garment to her sister and then moved back atop the bedspread. She folded her hands below her pregnant belly, wincing slightly as she made herself comfortable.

Minutes later, Kamaya stood in front of her full-length mirror. The all-white jumpsuit *was* cute and even cuter on her. The sleeveless, one-piece unit featured pant legs that tapered at the ankles and a slightly plunging neckline that gave it a slight hint of sexy. It was belted around the waist and it fit like a glove. She stepped into a pair of stylish suede pumps, then kicked them off in favor of a wedge heel for a more casual feel.

"What do you think?" she asked, turning to face her big sister.

"I think you look very pretty," Maitlyn said. "This Wesley guy is going to be blown away!"

Kamaya grinned. "He better be!" she muttered, as she pulled at her natural curls, insuring each was in perfect place. She leaned in closer to the mirror to inspect her face, swiping her index finger over one eyebrow and then the other. Her makeup was light, just enough to enhance her natural beauty. She'd underscored her eyes with a hint of eyeliner, and just the faintest touch of lip gloss coated her lips.

"You look great," Maitlyn reiterated. She quickly snapped a picture with her cell phone.

"What are you doing?" Kamaya said, her whole face frowning.

"You really don't think I'm going to let this moment go by and not share it with everyone, did you?"

"Maitlyn!"

The other woman laughed. "I only sent a text to Tarah and Katrina. But I'm sure Tarah will share it with the boys."

The doorbell suddenly resounded through the house, the soft chime resonating like church bells. As it did, the color drained from Kamaya's face.

"That's him! And I'm not ready!"

Maitlyn moved back onto her feet. "Yes, you are. I will go answer your door. Take a deep breath. Go pee one last time. Take another deep breath, then come say hello to your guy." She paused in the doorway. "And if you take too long, I'm going to regale him with stories about what you were like when we were kids."

"Don't do that."

"Don't make me," Maitlyn said, her grin wide and full, and then she turned, disappearing toward Kamaya's front door.

"Kamaya shouldn't be too long," Maitlyn said, as she gestured toward the living room sofa. "Please, have a seat. Can I get you something to drink?"

Wesley shook his head. "No, ma'am. I appreciate the offer, though."

Maitlyn smiled. "I'm not that much older than my sister. Please, call me Maitlyn."

Wesley nodded. "So you're the private investigator!"

"Is that what she told you?"

"She said if it exists, that you're the one who can find it."

The woman's laughter was warm and endearing. "I can be resourceful when I need to be."

"Your sister says it's more than that."

"My sister is too kind."

"I'm sure she has moments."

Maitlyn laughed. "I see that you're getting to know her well."

Wesley laughed with her, and their conversation continued for a few moments, the exchange easy and casual. He stole a quick glance down the length of hallway that he assumed led to the home's private spaces.

Maitlyn followed his gaze with one of her own. "She might be a minute. I hope you're not on a schedule."

"We're good with time," he said. He shook his head. "But I could use a big favor."

She stepped toward him, tossing her own look toward her sister's bedroom. After explaining what he needed, Maitlyn grinned. "Give me one minute," she said, disappearing out of his sight. She returned quickly, a small gym bag in hand. "Kamaya is touching up her makeup. She'll probably be in the bathroom for another ten minutes," she said, as she passed him the bag.

Wesley grinned. "Thanks. I'll run this to the car real quick."

He was back in the blink of an eye, no one but the two of them even knowing that he had left. He nodded his appreciation, whispering a soft thank-you.

Maitlyn winked at him. She rubbed a hand across her swollen belly.

"Congratulations! You and your husband must be very excited." Wesley tilted his head toward her bulging midsection.

"Thank you. We are. This is baby number three for us, our second son."

"Very nice. My mother says that sons are the key to every family's legacy and daughters are the locks."

"That's an interesting perspective."

"Crazy, old-school wisdom is what it is," he said, chuckling softly.

"Do you have any children, Wesley?"

"Do not answer that!" Kamaya admonished as she suddenly flounced into the room. "Really, Maitlyn?"

Her sister laughed, shrugging her narrow shoulders. "I was just making conversation."

Wesley moved onto his feet, turning to stare in Kamaya's direction. His eyes were wide and his mouth hung open ever so slightly. The woman was stunning and she took his breath away. "Hey!"

"Hi!" Kamaya chimed back, suddenly feeling awkward and nervous. She shifted her weight from one hip to the other.

"You look great!" he said softly.

"Thank you," she said, her own voice a loud whisper.

The two stood staring at each other as Maitlyn shifted her gaze between them like she was watching a tennis match. She suddenly laughed out loud, bemusement painting her expression.

"We should go," Kamaya said, moving to grab her purse. She shot her sister a look. "Lock my door when you leave, please."

Maitlyn nodded. She winked in Wesley's direction. "Take care of my sister. I know where to find you if anything happens to her," she said. "And my husband and brother both carry a badge and a gun!"

"Don't believe anything she told you about me," Kamaya stated as they walked the short length of her driveway toward Wesley's car.

He laughed. "What makes you think we talked about you?"

"Are you saying you didn't?" she retorted as she narrowed her gaze on him.

"I'm saying you shouldn't be so sensitive."

Kamaya changed the subject. "What year is your Toyota?"

"Why?"

"Because it looks like it might not make it. Maybe we should take my car."

"What's wrong with my ride?"

"Nothing. I just look cute in my heels and this outfit. If we were in gym clothes your car would be just fine. Since we're all dressed up my car might be a better fit."

"You don't look *that* cute," he said teasingly. "Besides, I never got the impression you were that pretentious. I'm actually surprised!"

Kamaya laughed. "I beg your pardon! I'll have you know I worked very hard to look this cute for you, and I am definitely not pretentious. It was only a suggestion. I'll save my gas. And if your clunker gives out on us, I'm not walking anywhere for help. I want to make sure that's clear."

They'd made it to his vehicle, and as he reached his arm around to open her door, his expression was smug.

There was a moment of hesitation as their gazes locked and held. The succulent scent of her perfume wafted past his nostrils. The fragrance reminded him of flowers brightened with a hint of citrus and warmed by the woodsy fragrances of amber and sandalwood. It was romantic and feminine and exceptionally memorable.

He took a deep breath. "Beautiful!" he whispered softly.

Kamaya's eyes widened even more. "I…oh…" she stammered, the comment throwing her off.

He shook his head. "Your perfume. You're wearing Beautiful by Estée Lauder."

"You recognize my perfume?"

"It's one of my favorites on a woman."

"I'm not even going to ask about the women you've been sniffing!" Kamaya said facetiously. She slid into the passenger seat.

Wesley chuckled to himself as he eased the door closed and moved around the front of the automobile to the driver's side. Once they were both settled comfortably, secured by their seat belts, he backed out of the driveway and headed toward the French Quarter.

"So, where are we going?" Kamaya asked.

"It's a surprise."

"I don't like surprises."

He grinned. "Why does that not surprise me!"

The look he gave her made her smile, unable to resist the sweet bend that pulled at her lips. Amusement danced across her face as she rolled her eyes.

"So, what's been going on since I last saw you?" Wesley asked, changing the subject as he maneuvered his car through the New Orleans streets.

"Business as usual. Fuel prices are dropping nicely

so we're seeing a very nice return on our investment. I'm even thinking about adding a few more gas stations to my portfolio."

Wesley shook his head. "Now that you got that out of your system, let me remind you of the rules. We are not going to talk about business."

"You really weren't serious about that, were you?"

"I was very serious. I said it and I meant it. No business."

"And if I break your little rule, what then?"

He cut an eye at her, mischief dancing in his eyes. "I will gladly paddle your backside, so don't test me."

"Ooh! Promises, promises! For all you know I might enjoy being paddled."

"Do you? Because I would gladly oblige you." There was a hint of something seductive and decadent in his banter.

Kamaya actually giggled, and she wasn't much of a giggler. A warm blush flooded her face. "So you're a pervert!"

Wesley chuckled. "Not at all. I just believe in insuring my partner is immensely satisfied, and if she wants to be spanked…well…" He winked at her and Kamaya felt moisture suddenly trickle, the heat between them rising with a vengeance.

Silence swallowed the space around them as they both reflected on that very brief exchange. The teasing had been filled with possibility, something about the flirtation feeling like plans in the making. The prospect of where that might take them suddenly had her even more excited.

Wesley pulled his car into a parking space near the New Orleans School of Cooking. He shut down the engine and turned in his seat to eye her directly. She looked around curiously, and it was only then that she spied the picnic basket in the backseat.

"So, we're having a picnic at the cooking school?"

He shook his head. "We are not. The basket is for later. Right now we're taking an interactive cooking class. I thought this would be fun since you don't cook."

"Excuse you! Who said I didn't know how to cook?"

"So, you do know how to cook?"

"That's beside the point. I just want to know who told you."

He laughed as he stepped out of the car and moved to the passenger side to open her door. He extended his hand toward her to help her out, and they both inhaled swiftly when skin touched skin, her palm sliding easily against his. He blew out a breath. "I told you before, I know how to read people. And I'm having a lot of fun reading you."

She pulled her hand from his. "Don't get it twisted, Wesley Walters. You are not reading me! You're only discovering what I want you to know!"

"If you say so," he answered as he tapped his palm against her backside.

The gesture was swift, stinging just enough to get her attention. It surprised her and Kamaya jumped ever so slightly. The look she gave him was priceless and Wesley chuckled heartily.

"Let's go cook!" he said, as he reached for her hand again, entwining his fingers between hers.

Kamaya nodded in agreement as she allowed him to pull her along beside him.

Kamaya couldn't remember the last time she'd had so much fun with a man. Once inside, they'd been introduced to Ms. Pat, the expert chef assigned to guide them. The grandmotherly woman was truly a treasure and a wealth of fun. After plying them with mimosas, she led them in the preparation of their meal. Together they learned about the history of and cultural influences on the cuisine they were cooking, Ms. Pat's stories were fodder for much hilarity in the classroom. Amidst an abundance of laughter, they cut, seasoned and prepared a complete meal, then sat down to enjoy the lunch they had just created.

The menu included a sweet potato and crab bisque, grillades, cheese grits and, for dessert, bananas Foster. The class lasted for almost three hours, and when they were finished neither wanted to leave the other's company. As they headed back to his car, Kamaya clutched a small bag of leftovers in one hand and held onto Wesley with her other hand. It was just past three o'clock and neither was ready for their afternoon to end.

"This has actually been a lot of fun," she said, as she leaned into his side. "Thank you!"

Wesley smiled. "You're very welcome. I'm glad you agreed to spend time with me. I've had a really good time, too!"

"So, where to now?" she asked, her enthusiasm spilling out of her eyes. "It's still early."

"I thought you'd be ready to call it a day. Don't you have to catch up on your rest to get ready for work on Monday?"

She came to an abrupt halt. "Hush your mouth! I thought we weren't talking any business."

Wesley laughed. "Is that what I just did?"

"You did. Looks like you're the one that wants to get spanked."

He shook his head. "Not my thing."

"Clearly you haven't met the right woman, then."

He grinned. "Now I'm intrigued."

"You should be," Kamaya whispered, as she pressed her palm to his chest, leaning her body against his.

Wesley felt every muscle in his body harden with desire and then she spun herself from him, a wicked laugh ringing through the evening air.

"So, where to now?" she asked again. "Or did you not have a contingency plan for when this date went really, really well?"

He chuckled. "Baby, I always have a contingency plan," he said matter-of-factly as he pointed at the picnic basket still resting on the backseat of his vehicle.

He moved to open the passenger door. As she eased her way inside, tossing him an amused look and the brightest smile, he tapped her on her ass one more time.

Chapter 7

The conversation between them wasn't anything either could have imagined. It was so much more, and both were enjoying the exchange. Kamaya was in awe of how easy it was to talk to Wesley. He had an attentive ear and he didn't take her too seriously. He asked questions that surprised her, the things he wanted to know about her making her heart sing. He respected her intelligence and seemed to genuinely appreciate those things she was enthusiastic about.

They talked politics, education, science and art. Wesley liked that she was opinionated and approached everything with a critical eye. Her mind was analytical and her actions methodical. She challenged his thinking, making him aware that not everything he believed was finite. And she was funny as hell, her ability to keep him laughing warming his spirit.

"So what do you have against men?" he asked, curiosity ringing in his tone.

Kamaya laughed. "I don't have anything against men. I love men. But I don't need to love them for long periods of time."

He tossed her a look, his head moving from side to side. "Do you purposely avoid long-term relationships?"

"I purposely avoid any relationship that does not make me happy."

"So I have a fighting chance?"

She laughed again. "You're doing okay."

"Just okay?"

"Are you feeling insecure? Because I don't do well with insecure men."

"Not at all. I just like to know where I stand with a woman. Like you, I don't want to waste any unnecessary time in a relationship that I know is going to fail."

"Well, right now you're doing good. You're getting all kinds of gold stars.

"So you know we're going to be magic together too?"

Her laugh was gut deep, tears misting at the edges of her eyes. "You're funny."

He smiled. "And I was trying to be serious!"

Her eyes danced from side to side as she scanned the landscape, enjoying the view. "What about you?" she finally asked. "What about your long-term relationships? Have you had any?"

He nodded. "I did. One. Everyone thought we were going to be married."

"What happened?"

"Irreconcilable differences. I wanted more out of life than she did. We were both smart enough to call it quits before we married and had kids and made a mess out of their lives."

"My parents have been married since forever. When, and if, I ever get married, I want what they have. I know I'm not an easy woman to get along with and I know that it's going to take a very special man to deal with me. I quickly eliminate those that don't make the cut because I still have hope that the right one will come along and sweep me off my feet."

He reached for her hand and gave her fingers a light squeeze. "I guess I arrived right on time," he said, his gaze connecting with hers.

Kamaya responded with an eye roll as she squeezed back. Her gaze shifted back outside.

Wesley drove until they were at the edge of Lake Ponchartrain, the largest inland body of water in Louisiana. Spanning some six hundred and thirty square miles, the lake was forty miles, west to east, and twenty-four miles from south to north. Their destination was the New Orleans Yacht Club.

"I hope you like the water," he said casually.

Kamaya hesitated briefly. "As long as we're not skinny-dipping or anything like that, I think I'll be good!"

He chuckled. "I thought I'd save the skinny-dipping for our second date."

"I am not that kind of girl!" she exclaimed. "Maybe the third date. And only if you're lucky."

He grinned. "I don't need luck. I am exceptionally skilled. You'll be surprised at what I'm going to be able to talk you out of, including your clothes," he said with a deep laugh.

Kamaya rolled her eyes as they exited the car. She

didn't bother to respond, knowing that he probably wasn't far from being right.

Wesley nodded, his smug expression blooming across his face for a second time. "I have a sailboat that I keep anchored here. I thought it might be nice to just sit and relax, and maybe enjoy a bottle of wine or two. Later on, after the sun sets, there's going to be fireworks. If we're still here, we'll have ringside seats."

"*If* we're still here?"

"I can't assume that just because I'm enjoying our time together, that you'll want to stay. I'm prepared to take you home when you're ready."

"So you're not that exceptionally skilled?" She gave him her own smug look, laughter shimmering in her dark eyes. "Because I would think that if you could talk me out of my clothes, talking me into hanging around a little longer would be a piece of cake."

Wesley nodded, laughing heartily. "You're funny, Kamaya Boudreaux."

"Not nearly as hilarious as you are, Wesley Walters!" She took a deep breath as she assessed her surroundings. The sky was a brilliant shade of Carolina blue. There wasn't a cloud to be seen and the sun was gleaming brilliantly. The water shimmered beneath the light, and it couldn't have been a better day for them to enjoy being on the water. Kamaya was suddenly even more excited about the prospect of spending that time with Wesley in such a beautiful environment.

The sixty-five-foot custom, twin-keel cruiser was tied at the end of the lengthy, wooden planked dock. The sailboat had an enclosed pilothouse that had been designed for comfortable, long-term water cruising. It was an all-weather, go-anywhere vessel that could easily be handled by two people. Wesley took great pride in pointing out the new teak deck, the renovated interior layout that included a master cabin and second guest cabin aft, a forward guest cabin, a saloon and a galley. The luxury finishes and upscale fixtures made it a sight to behold.

"This is very nice!" Kamaya exclaimed as she spun around in slow, tight circle, taking it all in.

Wesley nodded. "It's where I retreat to when I need to clear my mind," he said, as he moved toward the galley to drop the picnic basket. Turning toward her, he held out the small gym bag that Kamaya's sister had packed for him.

Kamaya eyed it and him with a raised brow. "That's mine. Where did you…" she started.

"Your sister is *very resourceful*. We both figured you might want a change of clothes," he said, as he passed the carrier into her hands. "I'm not sure what's inside, but I asked her to pack something you wouldn't mind getting dirty. Just in case." He pointed toward the master bedroom. "You can change in there."

"I can't believe you already have my family plotting against me."

He laughed. "I prefer to see it as Maitlyn plotted *with* me on your behalf."

Kamaya shook her head. "Just wait until I get my hands on her."

He took a step toward her, closing the space between them. He brushed the backs of his fingers against her cheek, sliding stray curls from her face. "Be nice to your sister. I owe her."

His touch suddenly had Kamaya heated. A response caught deep in her chest and she could only nod. She took an abrupt step back, and then she turned, practically racing toward the bedroom and the door she could close tightly between them.

Once inside, Kamaya dropped down onto the bed and sucked in air. Her reaction to the nearness of him had been unexpected. And intense. There was a low throbbing that had begun to beat between her legs, her sweet spot seeming to cry out for attention. And release. She sighed, her wanting suddenly feeling like a weight around her body that she couldn't escape.

She had no words to explain what she was feeling. It was something more than sexual desire. Something that was completely foreign to her. Whatever it was needed to be contained and extinguished, and she suddenly fathomed that giving in to her carnal urgings might happen tonight. But playing where she did business was never a good idea, and although she really liked Wesley, she couldn't cross that boundary. Or could she?

She shook the garments from the bag, curious to see what Maitlyn had packed. A pair of denim shorts, her favorite Bob Marley T-shirt and flip-flops fell onto the bed. Maitlyn had gotten it right, Kamaya thought, as she reached inside to make sure there was nothing else left to unpack. And then she laughed, her head shaking as she pulled out the satin-and-lace teddy tucked down into the bottom corner. Maitlyn had a sense of humor and Kamaya couldn't help but be amused.

Wesley was topside when Kamaya finally reappeared. He had changed his clothes, as well, his suit replaced by chino shorts, a Polo shirt and boat shoes. He was readying the boat to sail, inspecting all the standing rigging—the cables and ropes that supported the mast and the turnbuckles and cotter pins that secured the rigging to the hull. He explained everything as he did it, and Kamaya was anxious to take it all in. It was only minutes later that they were headed out of the channel into the open waters.

"How do you know where to steer around the other boats?" she asked, genuinely interested.

"You have to honor the navigational buoys. They tell you where the water is safe and where it isn't. When you leave a marina, the red buoys are always left to port."

Pointing the boat into the wind they hoisted the sails and then it was as if they were running with the late afternoon air. Kamaya instantly understood the attraction to the sport. Watching Wesley, she could see just how smitten he was. Everything about sailing excited him, and she was thoroughly engaged as he educated her on sailing terminology and boat parts. It took no time at all before she was just as enthusiastic already plotting to perhaps buy her own boat.

"Watch the boom!" Wesley hollered.

Kamaya ducked as the horizontal support swung over her head, the boat shifting directions as Wesley turned it around. They sailed for a good two hours before heading back into the marina, returning to the dock. When the boat was tied in place, the sails lowered and the anchor dropped, Kamaya threw her arms round his neck and hugged him tightly. "That was so much fun!" she exclaimed.

Wesley hugged her back, holding her close as he savored the nearness of her. She felt like she'd been made especially for his arms and when she stepped back he didn't want to let her go. "I'm glad you had a good time," he said softly, as he pulled her hand to his lips and kissed the back of her fingers. "Are you hungry? You've really been working hard."

"I am a little munchie. I think lunch is definitely gone! Are you going to teach me how to cook on the open water next?"

He laughed. "No. I'm going to show you how to put cheese and crackers on a plate," he teased.

"Now that sounds like it would take exceptional skill," she said facetiously.

Wesley grinned, guiding her down to the lower level of the boat. As she made herself comfortable on the cushioned sofa, he unpacked goodies from the picnic basket. There were crackers and cheese, pepperoni and salami, a container of fresh berries, cookies and a bottle of Moscato. He plated the food and poured them both a glass of wine, and then he joined her.

"So, how long have you been sailing?" Kamaya asked, as she pulled one leg beneath her bottom.

"I did a private party many years ago for a woman who was celebrating her fiftieth birthday with her girl-friends. She had a sailboat and we sailed down to Key West. The crew she'd hired taught me everything and I was hooked from then on. I bought my own boat two years later, and I've been sailing regularly ever since."

Kamaya nodded. She swallowed a bite of cheese and pepperoni. "So, did you do a lot of private parties when you were dancing?" she asked.

He shifted his gaze in her direction. "There were a few."

She took a gulp of her wine and then a second. An awkward silence swept between them.

Wesley dropped his own glass to the wooden coffee

table in front of them. "If you want to ask me something, just do so."

She shook her head. "Nope!" She gulped again. "I have no questions that need to be asked."

"Well, I have a question for you."

They locked eyes as he turned to face her, leaning forward to rest both elbows on his thighs, his hands clasped tightly together. "Is there something going on between you and Paxton? I noticed some tension between you two that day you came to the club. A little lover's spat, maybe?"

Kamaya took a deep breath as she suddenly snatched her eyes from his. She leaned to rest her own drink on the table. Of all the questions she'd been prepared for, she hadn't expected to be asked that one. Over the years she'd had to explain her relationship with Paxton more than once, her family, especially, always having questions. And over the years she had always lied, not wanting to share the truth of her friendship with the man. But now it was Wesley asking and she couldn't lie.

"We're friends. We *were* friends with benefits but he recently became engaged to someone I don't particularly care for and the benefits portion of our friendship ended."

"Are you in love with him?"

Kamaya paused, that question surprising her as well. "We've been friends since forever, so, yes, I love him. But I'm not *in* love with him. What we had was just convenient during a time in our lives when we needed convenience."

"And you're sure that you're done and finished with the *benefits* portion of your relationship?"

"Without any doubts!"

"Is there anyone *else* I need to be concerned about?"

She smiled. "You didn't need to be concerned about Paxton. But, no, there are no more friends with benefits in my life at that moment."

He nodded. "So I'll answer the question you didn't want to ask. No, I don't dance privately anymore. And I've never dated nor been involved with anyone that I have ever performed for."

Kamaya gave him an eye roll. "That wasn't my question."

His eyebrows lifted slightly. "It wasn't?"

She shook her head. "No. I was going to ask, if you and I were dating, could I look forward to a private lap dance. *That* was *my* question."

Wesley laughed. "I am interested in dating you, but I'll be honest, I'm worried how that might affect our business together. I'm sure it's crossed your mind, as well."

Kamaya took a breath. "So no lap dances, is that what you're saying?"

He shook his head, amusement dancing across his face. "Until we figure out where this is going we might want to just take things slow."

"I wasn't rushing anything," she said matter-of-factly.

He nodded. "You're right. You weren't. I think I just got a little ahead of myself. It won't happen again."

She blew a soft sigh. "Well, that's no fun!" she said, her tone dripping with sarcasm.

Wesley shifted closer toward her. He reached for her hand and held it, gazing directly into her eyes. As Kamaya stared back she could feel herself falling headfirst into the look he was giving her, something earnest and fantastical lost deep in his dark eyes. She found herself searching for something that belonged only to her.

The moment was heated and she realized her breath was coming in short gasps. She bit down against her bottom lip as she closed her own eyes, trying to reel in each breath. She felt his face next to hers and then his warm breath blowing softly across her skin as he whispered softly into her ear. "But the answer to your question would be yes," he said. "And only for you!"

Wesley was grateful for the cool breezes blowing off the waters of Lake Ponchartrain. After responding to Kamaya's question, he stood up, moving onto his feet abruptly as he needed to put some space between them. He refilled both their wine glasses and then invited her topside to get ready for the fireworks.

He was glad Kamaya had taken a brief moment to herself, her own emotions surely running as high as his. Neither had actually voiced what they were feeling, but if he were honest, Wesley had to admit that he wanted her, and he wanted her more than he'd ever wanted any woman before. It had taken every ounce of his fortitude to contain the rise of nature that had threatened to grow full and abundant for attention.

He stared out to the water and the sun that was just beginning to set on the horizon. It would only be a matter of minutes before the fiery orb kissed the line of blue moisture. Music was playing in the distance, one of the other boat owners sharing his sound system. The Latin tunes were melodic and playful, and fitting for the moment. Someone else agreed, a man's voice calling out. "Hey, Bernard! If no one else minds, can you turn it up?"

"Please, turn it up!" someone else echoed from a boat on the other side.

Minutes later the music's volume vibrated warmly and a round of applause echoed with appreciation. Wesley smiled as Kamaya came into view, giving him a slight wave of her hand.

"Is it a party?" she asked, her body swaying in rhythm with a salsa beat.

"It is definitely a celebration," he said.

She shook her hips from side to side, the exaggerated gesture making him laugh. Holding out both hands, Kamaya gestured for him to join her. "Come salsa with me!" she said, her face shimmering with joy.

He shook his head as she pulled him to his feet. He slid his right hand around her upper shoulder and clasped her hand with his left. With little effort they were moving in near perfect sync with each other, their bodies twisting and spinning together like a well-oiled machine. Wesley was impressed with how completely comfortable she was, her body movements graceful and seductive. She was enjoying herself, and the sheer beauty of that was written all over her face and in each motion of her body.

"You are very good," he said, as he spun her in a tight circle against him and then away.

Kamaya grinned. "Thank you!" she said as they moved from one side of the boat to the other.

When the song ended there was another round of applause, and for the first time Kamaya realized the family on the boat beside them had been watching. She laughed as she tossed Wesley a look and then they both took a bow. Wesley's neighbor gave them two thumbs-up before turning his attention back to his wife and kids.

Kamaya and Wesley took a seat as energy continued to vibrate between them. It was electrical, shimmering with an effervescence that was completely magical. The intensity of it surprised them both.

"That was so much fun," Kamaya said, breaking the blanket of silence that had descended over them.

"It *was* fun. And you surprised me. You have serious dance skills."

"Five years of Latin dance lessons. You should see me rumba!"

Before Wesley could respond, a flash of white light burst in the sky above their heads. Kamaya grinned, clapping her hands together. She was giddy with excitement, her reaction almost childlike.

The lights continued to burst, fireworks snapping, crackling and popping with a vengeance. She shifted her body against his, the two of them settling comfortably against each other. Wesley draped an arm over her shoulders and pulled her close as she leaned her head against his shoulder. They both stared toward the darkened sky.

The fireworks exploded. The moment was enchanting and Kamaya couldn't remember the last time she'd felt so carefree and relaxed. When the last burst of light flashed a brilliant shade of red, green and yellow, she snuggled against Wesley and his body reacted.

The music was still sounding through the air, soft and easy, stringed instruments playing a sweet jazz tune. Kamaya sat upright, shifting forward in her seat. Her mind was suddenly racing, her heart beating rapidly in her chest.

"Are you okay?" Wesley asked, concern registering in his tone.

She turned her body to face him. Her head moved up and down. "Everything is perfect," she whispered, as she eased herself up and over his body, straddling her legs around him.

"I thought we were going to take things slow?" he said, as his arms wrapped around her waist, one hand clutching her buttocks, the other skating across her back.

Kamaya whispered. "This is slow." And then she kissed him, dropping her mouth against his.

Chapter 8

It took only a split second for Kamaya to know what she wanted and she knew she wanted Wesley. In that split second she'd been able to weigh the pros and cons of taking their relationship to the next level, and without an ounce of hesitation she'd taken that first step.

Her lips glided like silk across his lips, capturing his mouth possessively. She abandoned every one of her inhibitions as she wrapped her arms around him, pressing her pelvis against the rise of nature in his shorts. She wanted him, the need just shy of desperate, but everything about it felt right. She pulled her mouth from his, panting heavily as they both gasped for air.

"Are you sure about this?" he whispered, his hands still dancing over her ass and hips.

She responded by kissing him again. Her tongue probed against his lips until he allowed her access to his mouth, meeting her tongue with his own. There were an entanglement of hot breath and the sweet taste of the wine they'd shared. He took that as a yes.

Wesley held her tightly as he shifted forward and moved onto his feet, lifting her into his arms. Kamaya wrapped her legs around his waist as they continued to exchange a long, lustful kiss that left them both breathless. His hand cupped the perfect round of her ass and squeezed each firm cheek as he pulled her tighter against him.

As if he did it regularly, he maneuvered them from topside to the deck below, away from the prying eyes of those still sitting beneath the late-night stars. He carried her easily back to the bedroom, careful not to bump into any of the furniture along the way.

When he made it to the edge of the bed, Wesley eased her down onto the covers, his mouth moving from her lips to her neck as he left a trail of damp kisses along the way. Her skin was salty and sweet against his tongue and he lapped at her as if doing so would quench his thirst. He nipped at her flesh, biting her gently, and when he did she clutched him even closer to her.

He suddenly stood upright, pulling his shirt over his head. Kamaya gasped at the sight of his bare chest. His skin was melted chocolate, decadent and deliciously sweet. It was satin softness pulled taut over hardened steel, each sinewy muscle constricted. She reached a hand out to touch him and her fingers quivered with anticipation, each digit heated as every one of her synapses fired.

She rose up onto her knees and gently pressed her hand over his heart. She could feel it beating against her palm like a college drumline, and as if she'd willed it, her own heartbeat synced perfectly with his. The moment made them both gasp.

Reaching for her, Wesley pulled at her T-shirt, the image of Bob Marley on the front proclaiming One Love. She lifted her arms obligingly, the soft pant of her breath moving his temperature to rise. He pulled her back into his arms and reclaimed her mouth, kissing her hungrily. With little effort, he undid the hooks and eyes on the lace bra she wore, easing the straps gently off her shoulders. Her skin was sheer perfection, unblemished and the creamiest caramel color. His hands danced over the soft lines, his mouth following where his fingers led.

With her breasts exposed, Kamaya suddenly felt vulnerable and feared it might be reflected in her eyes. Tears misted behind the lids and she gasped, holding tight to the breath she'd taken. Wesley hugged her to him, seemingly sensing the rise of her anxiety, and just like that it was gone. She kissed him, her mouth tasting his as his hands trailed over her back.

Wesley palmed her bare breasts, his touch burning sweetly against her skin. Her nipples had hardened, nubs of dark candy cradled against the round pools of her chocolate areola. He gently rubbed and twisted and pinched her nipples between his thick fingers. Pulling his mouth from her he sucked one breast and then the other, suckling at her with a voracity that surprised them both.

Kamaya threw her head back, the sensations sweeping through her entire body. "Oh, yes!" she exclaimed, the words blowing like a loud hiss past her lips.

She reached between them, sliding both hands into his shorts. His cock was engorged, the weight of it heavy and full. When she wrapped her fingers around him, he felt his erection stiffen more than he would have thought possible. His girth surprised her and her eyes snapped downward to stare.

Pulling himself from her, Wesley pushed his shorts past his ass and down to his ankles. He kicked them away, then stood in all his glory, the magnificence of his grandeur taking her breath away. She reached for him again, pulling at his member fervently. Wesley moaned, the seductive groan echoing through the room. He stood with his arms folded up and above his head as she stroked him over and over again.

Kamaya suddenly took him into her mouth, sucking him in with one swift inhale of air. She licked up and down his shaft, her tongue sweeping over the tip and head of his member. He moaned a second time, the intensity of the sensations causing him to quiver with excitement. He whispered her name, the repetition a soft chant encouraging her ministrations.

He swore, the profanity a contradiction to how he usually expressed himself. "That feels so good!" he murmured.

The vulgarity made her smile as she continued to pleasure him with her mouth. "Do you like that?" she asked, as she went back to stroking him and softly lapping at his balls.

"Oh, yes!" he muttered, air catching deep in his chest. He began to shake, muscle spasms firing from the sheer power of her touch. He suddenly grabbed her hands and lifted her chin, pulling himself from her. "Don't make me come yet!" he said, his head moving from side to side.

Kamaya sat back on her haunches, the seductive smile on her face like a beacon, calling him to her.

"Lie back," he commanded, desire glowing in the look he gave her.

Kamaya dropped her torso back against the mattress, pulling her legs from beneath her. He pulled at her denim shorts, tugging them and the thong she wore from around her body. Crawling up onto the bed Wesley knelt between her thighs, spreading her long limbs open. Kamaya clutched her breasts in her hands as she drew her knees up toward her shoulders, the gesture inviting.

That smug grin she'd grown to love danced across his face as they locked eyes for a brief second, and then he dropped his mouth to her entrance, licking her fervently. Kamaya clutched at the bedding, drawing the bedspread into her tightened fists. She closed her eyes, her lids clenched tightly together, pleasure sweeping over her expression.

She pressed a palm against the back of his head as his thick tongue lashed at her clit repeatedly. Her hips rose from the bed as she pressed herself into his mouth. The moment was everything she had fantasized and more. Her body suddenly shook, control completely lost as the first orgasm hit and hit hard. Her torso lurched and her back arched. Kamaya screamed.

She was still shaking and quivering as he sheathed himself with a condom, the prophylactic seeming to appear out of nowhere. She'd been so lost in the pleasure rushing through her body that she must've missed him reaching into a nearby drawer to find the protection.

He lined himself up at the entrance of her most private place and slowly pressed himself forward. She was wet and he entered her easily, her body eagerly welcoming him inside. Her muscles clutched and pulled at him, drawing him deeper into her wetness.

He was exceptionally long and thick, and he filled her, her pelvis feeling full and complete, and just when she thought she couldn't take much more, her body surprised her, opening itself further, refusing to let him go.

They moved in sync, the pulling and pushing steady and intense. He stroked her over and over again, holding tight to her torso as she clutched him, her thin arms wrapped around his back and shoulders.

"Harder!" she screamed, her lush voice a profusion of pure lust. She grabbed his hips and pulled him even deeper into her. "Oh, yes!" she cried out. "Harder, baby! Harder!"

Wesley intensified the pace of his thrusts and she pushed upward to meet him. The feverish pitch of their moans and groans was a symphony of its own making and they played each other like finely tuned instruments. He picked up the pace, his strokes relentless as he drove himself in and out of her.

"I'm going to cum!" she moaned. "I'm going to…" Kamaya suddenly tensed and let out another scream of pure ecstasy.

"That's it! Give it to me, baby!" he gasped.

Their two bodies were a juxtaposition of arms and legs flailing, and then, with a few last thrusts, he exploded inside of her. He screamed with her, his own orgasm bursting forth with a vengeance. He continued to push and pull himself in and out of her, her tight vaginal walls milking him dry, and then he collapsed on top of her.

Kamaya lay beneath him, breathless. He trailed light

kisses over her neck and along the curve of her chin, then pressed his lips to her lips one last time before rolling his body from hers.

Side by side they lay together, still holding tightly to each other's hands. Sweat dripped from his brow, perspiration bubbling from her pores as they gasped for air, waiting for their breathing to return to a semblance of normalcy. As they settled into the aftermath of their loving, Wesley turned his head to face her, meeting her stare with one of his own.

"I'm never letting you go," he whispered, and then he drifted off into a deep sleep.

Kamaya smiled as she closed her own eyes. She'd been thinking the very same thing.

When Wesley opened his eyes again, it was just past midnight. The boat was rocking gently from side to side, the peaceful sway soothing. Kamaya was still sleeping soundly, the expression on her face angelic. He rose slowly, mindful not to disrupt her from her rest. He knew she was tired and he didn't want to wake her. He also didn't want to risk her wanting to leave him.

The tide turning on their relationship had caught them both by surprise. He couldn't begin to tell her or anyone how much he had wanted to kiss her since he'd first laid eyes on her. So, when she'd taken the leap he'd been more than ready to catch her. There had only been a very brief second when he could have walked away, pretending the moment hadn't happened, and when she'd given him permission to continue, their happy ending had been written in gold.

His desire for Kamaya had been intense, nothing and no one able to keep him from her. He brushed his fingers lightly down the profile of her face, pushing her hair back against the pillow. She was exquisite, everything about her moved his spirit. As he thought about her, and them together, he suddenly realized that she had his heart and she didn't even know it.

He eased his way to the restroom and emptied his bladder. After a quick wash and dry he moved back into the bedroom. Kamaya sat upright in his bed, her knees pulled up to her chest.

"Hey, I didn't mean to wake you."

"You didn't. I missed you. It was cold."

He nodded. The outside temperature had dropped substantially. He moved to the closet and reached inside for two extra blankets.

Kamaya rose from the bed and disappeared into the bathroom. When she returned, Wesley had already crawled back into the bed and was sitting up beneath the extra blankets waiting for her. She snuggled her way back to him, to steal his surplus heat. As she cradled her bottom into the recess of his crotch he spooned himself around her, locking his arms tightly around her waist.

"I wasn't planning on spending the night," she said.

He laughed. "Neither was I. I sleep on the boat all the time, but you're the only woman who's ever joined me."

"Ohhh, I must be special!"

"Exceptionally! But if you want me to take you home..."

She shook her head, pulling his arms tighter around her waist. "No. I am home" she said, her voice a loud whisper, her comment bold. But it was honest, the feelings as intense as anything she'd ever felt before.

Wesley placed a damp kiss against the nape of her neck. Everything about the moment felt good, and nat-

ural, as if they were both right where they were supposed to be. She felt perfect in his arms and he suddenly
wondered what it would be like when she was no longer
there. He marveled at how quickly he'd gotten comfortable with the idea of her being with him. She seemed
to read his thoughts as she nestled herself even closer
against him.

They could hear the water lapping gently at the sides
of the boat. The wind had picked up, the side-to-side
vibration lulling them both into a state of quiet bliss.
As they thought about each other and where they found
themselves, neither had the words to express what they
were feeling. So neither said anything preferring instead
to just settle into the comfort of each other's touch.

Body heat pushed their temperatures up nicely. Lying
together neither felt the chill in the air. Kamaya made no
move to pull herself from him when she felt his growing excitement press against her buttocks. Instead, she
bent forward at the waist, curling her behind closer
against him. She lifted her leg ever so slightly, his erection sliding past the crack of her ass to settle between
her warm thighs.

Kamaya began to rock back and forth slowly, her
body stroking him obscenely. He felt himself swell and
thicken even more, unable to resist the intensity of her
touch. He suddenly felt her fingers tapping at him, the
pad of her index finger drawing tight circles over the
head of his member. He reached around to press his
hands between her legs, finding her fingers darting
back and forth between him and her clit.

He stroked her gently until her breathing became
labored. She was wanting more, and so was he. He
reached over for a condom and sheathed himself

quickly. He pushed his hand between them to lift her leg higher. His hips shifted forward against her, sliding along the damp crack of her ass. He eased past the wrinkled rosebud toward the deeper, wetter, hotter depression that marked her sacred place.

When she gave a little wiggle of her hips and a backward push that took his breath away, he entered her in one swift motion. Kamaya moved her hips in slow circles as he worked himself in and out of her. His hands clutched her hips, gently pulling her back and forth against the length of his cock until his pelvis pushed tight against her bare skin.

One of his hands slid into the length of her hair, the loose curls wrapping around his fingers. The other trailed around her hip, coming to rest atop the flat of her stomach. He caressed her, the skin beneath his touch like puffs of cotton. His hand danced from her stomach to her breasts and back, eventually sinking lower between her legs to tease her clit as he continued to drive himself in and out of her. He rode her buttocks and hips, loving her slowly, in and out, grinding himself against her backside.

They fell from bliss together, dropping into an abyss of sheer pleasure. She orgasmed, muttering his name over and over again as if she were in prayer. The pulsing sensation of her body were like a vice around his, igniting his explosion. His orgasm ripped through his body as if he'd combusted from the inside out. Something like a whimper reverberated out of his mouth.

When the shaking stopped and the tremors ceased, she whispered his name.

"Yes, baby?"

"If we're going to keep doing this all night, you're going to need to feed me," she said.

Wesley laughed. "Are we doing this all night?"

"Oh, hell, yeah!"

Chapter 9

A hint of daylight gleamed through the small window. Kamaya opened one eye as Wesley nuzzled his face into her hair. His naked body lay partially atop hers, one leg tossed over hers, an arm wrapped around her waist. She had no idea what time it was, but she did know she wasn't yet ready to face the new day.

She'd lost count of the number of times he had brought her to orgasm, but the achy throbbing in her sweet spot was a reminder of all they'd shared. She shifted even closer to him, wanting to feel the weight of him against her.

"Good morning," he mumbled, his warm breath blowing past her ear.

"Five more minutes," she muttered back, groaning softly. "I just need five more minutes."

Wesley chuckled. "That's good. I need at least another hour. Maybe two."

"It's all your fault," she said. "You kept us up all night."

"No, no, no! I am not taking the blame! You are insatiable!"

"Says the man with the perpetual hard-on!"

He laughed again. "Like I said, that's on you. You do that to me. I'm hard now!"

Kamaya giggled as she turned to face him, adjusting the pillow beneath her head. "That sounds like a personal problem. Go back to sleep. Maybe it'll go away," she said, as she reached down between them to wrap her hand around his manhood.

He was hard, the organ pulsing slightly, his flesh heated. He kissed her forehead, a wide smile on his face as he closed his eyes, savoring the sensation of her fingers gripping him tightly.

A few minutes passed, but just as they were about to doze off again, Wesley's cell phone vibrated loudly.

"And that would be my mother," he said, before he even bothered to look at the caller ID. He reached for the device and answered it, putting the phone on speaker as Kamaya released the hold she had on him.

"Hey, Mama!"

"Good morning, baby! Were you sleeping?"

"No, ma'am," he answered, the little white lie spilling from his mouth.

Kamaya smiled.

"You sound like you were asleep. Don't be telling me no fibs, Wesley!"

"I was just talking with my new friend. She's about to make me breakfast," he responded.

Kamaya lifted herself slightly, eyeing him with amusement.

His mother continued. "Oh? Is this new friend that young lady you were telling me about?"

"Yes, ma'am. I hope to introduce you to her when you and Daddy come to visit."

Kamaya's brow lifted upon learning that he had discussed her with his parents.

"Well, you know I can't wait! If you have finally met a young woman you want your daddy and I to meet, she must be very special!"

Wesley winked at Kamaya as he changed the subject. "You and Daddy okay this morning?"

"We're just fine. We just got back from church."

Wesley looked at his wristwatch. "Church? This early?"

"We went to the eight o'clock service. Your daddy wanted to be out before Sunday school. He and Mr. Jeffries are going fishing this afternoon."

"That sounds like fun." Wesley feigned a yawn, tapping his hand over his mouth. The gesture made Kamaya giggle softly.

"Are you and your friend going to Sunday service?"

"I don't think so."

"She does go to church, doesn't she? Didn't you say she goes to church?"

"Hold on. Let me ask her." He cupped his hand over the phone receiver. "You do go to church, don't you?"

Kamaya laughed. "Yes! I'm a good Catholic girl. I go to Mass on a regular basis."

"Just checking." He resumed his conversation. "She goes, Mama. She's a good girl."

"Uh-huh!"

"She is!"

"If you say so, son, I'm sure she is."

Kamaya shook her head, her eyes rolling.

"Well, I just called to check on you before I go see about Ms. Alice."

"What happened to Ms. Alice?" he questioned, referring to the old woman who lived across the street from his parents.

"Poor thing broke her hip yesterday. That no-good husband of hers ain't no kind of help, so I need to make sure she's okay."

"I'm sorry to hear that. Please tell her I'm thinking about her."

"I sure will. Are you ready to pray with me, baby?"

"Hold on. Let me put you on speaker so my friend can pray with us."

"Boy, I know you already had me on speaker!"

Kamaya's eyes widened as Wesley stifled a laugh. He ignored his mother's comment.

"Kamaya, say hello to my mother. Mama, this is Kamaya Boudreaux."

Kamaya sat herself upright. She gave him a swift punch in the arm. "Good morning, Mrs. Walters."

"Good morning, Kamaya. Ain't that a pretty name!"

"Thank you."

"Have you and Wesley been seeing each other long?"

Wesley interjected. "Let's pray, Mama!"

He grabbed Kamaya's hand, kissing the backs of her fingers before entwining his own between hers. He lowered his head and closed his eyes. Kamaya eyed him as his mother began to pray.

"Father God, we come to give You thanks this morning for Your many blessings, Lord. Thank You for allowing us to rise to see this new day. We pray that You give us strength today, to be strong from the temptations that may come our way. You know our struggles, Father God, and we pray that You will be with us as we go through them. Carry us, Lord if we are weak. If we stumble, please, forgive us. Lead us from evil, so that we may serve You well. We praise You, Father! For without You, we would not be where we are or have the strength that we have. Bless our loved ones and keep them close to You that they will also know Your will. And please, Lord, bless this union between my son Wesley and his new friend Kamaya, that it will be pleasing in Your eyes. In Your Son Jesus's name, we pray, Amen."

"Amen," Wesley and Kamaya both echoed.

"Kamaya, I look forward to meeting you, dear," Mrs. Walters concluded.

"Thank you. Your son has told me so much about you, so I look forward to meeting you, as well."

"Wesley, call your daddy later this evening. Ask him about his new fishing pole."

"I will. I love you."

"Mama loves you too, baby! Goodbye, Kamaya!"

After he disconnected the call, Wesley leaned to kiss Kamaya's lips, gently pressing his mouth against hers. "My mother likes you," he said.

"Your mother doesn't know I'm lying here naked in your bed."

"Oh, she knew! She just didn't say anything. Trust me. My mother doesn't miss a thing!"

"She sounds like my mother! Boy are we in for it!"

"They're both a blessing! I know I wouldn't give that old woman away for anything in this world."

"You're a mama's boy!"

"And damn proud of it!

Kamaya leaned to kiss him again. "One day I hope I have a son who feels the same way about me. I know that's how my brothers feel about our mother."

"So you do want children?"

"Did you think I didn't?"

Wesley shook his head. "I really don't know what to think. That's why I asked."

She nodded. "I do. One day. I don't know if I'm really ready yet, and I might be running out of time, but I do want a family. A husband, children, a dog! Other people dwell on it more than I do, though. I know it will happen when it's supposed to happen. And it has to happen in that order or my mother will kill me!"

He wrapped his arms around her, hugging her close. "I want three kids. Maybe even four. A house full of boys!"

"I was thinking more like one."

"I'll meet you in the middle. Two. One boy and one girl. And I think we should get to practicing right now!" he said. "That way you can be pregnant right after the honeymoon and make both our mothers very happy!"

Kamaya wore amusement across her face like perfectly placed makeup. "As long as you get that I have to be married first!"

"Hey, my mother is a card-carrying Baptist. I understand completely! Like I said, it would just be practice for the real thing."

Kamaya laughed as he lifted the covers to peer down at his rising erection. "That thing looks deadly!" she mused.

He grinned. "It is. Baby, this right here will kill you with love!"

* * *

Kamaya had ignored the first five phone calls from her sister, sending them right to voice mail. When Wesley's cell phone suddenly rang and Maitlyn's number flashed across the screen, she had to answer. She shook her head as he passed her his device.

"Why are you calling me on Wesley's telephone?"

"Because you didn't answer yours and we needed to make sure you're still alive!" Maitlyn responded.

Her sisters all chimed in with their hellos.

"You're all on the line?"

"Please, you had a date and you didn't think we would call to find out how it went?" Maitlyn asked sarcastically.

"Where are you?" Katrina questioned.

Kamaya blew a soft sigh. "Wesley and I are spending the day on his sailboat."

"You're still on his boat?" Maitlyn asked. "Maybe I should have packed you more clothes! Did you wear that nightie I tossed in?"

Kamaya laughed. "I'm wearing it now," she said glibly.

"You had sex with the stripper?" Tarah chimed in. "You go, girl! I saw that video!"

Kamaya shook her head. "Really, Maitlyn?"

"What did I do?"

"Can you keep anything to yourself?"

The women laughed.

"Like you don't know the answer to that!" Tarah said teasingly. "Now you know what it feels like having everyone all up in your business!"

"I expected better from you, Tarah."

"Nope! Payback is real!"

"At least I didn't tell your brothers," Maitlyn said.

Wesley was eyeing Kamaya curiously, amusement dancing over his face. He turned the page of the newspaper he was reading, pretending to be interested in one of the articles on the sports page.

"Well, I'm good. Wesley's good. We're both fine. There's no need for you to worry about me. I will call you all later."

"Not so fast," Maitlyn chimed. "Senior has to have a colonoscopy on Tuesday. Can you take the old people and be there to sit with Mom?"

"Can't Kendrick do it?

"Kendrick asked if you could do it. He and Vanessa are going out of town."

Kamaya blew a soft sigh. "I guess so. As long as you didn't schedule it for some ridiculous hour in the morning."

"Senior scheduled his own appointment. He has to be at the hospital at seven-thirty."

"He does this to me on purpose. You do know that, right?"

"Your father does it to all of us on purpose. You're not special," Katrina responded with a light chuckle.

"When are you coming home?" Maitlyn asked. "You cannot spend another night with your new boyfriend. You already look like you're fast!"

"I do not!"

"It is just a little trashy," Katrina interjected.

"It was first-date sex. That makes you look *really* trashy," Tarah noted.

"Tch," Kamaya sucked her teeth. "Like y'all have never done it before. Don't get me started."

"We're not talking about us right now," Maitlyn said, chuckling. "We're talking about you."

"I have never done that!" Katrina exclaimed. "The one time I even thought about doing it, your mother did a drive-by! Talk about a buzz kill!"

The sisters all laughed.

"Mama says a man won't marry fast and easy!" Tarah giggled. "But I feel you, girl! Get your groove on, big sister!"

"He's a stripper! Are you really thinking about marrying a stripper?" Katrina questioned.

"He's a *former* stripper!" Maitlyn clarified. "Get your facts straight or she'll be mad at me for passing along misinformation."

"I'm mad at you anyway," Kamaya noted. "But we'll talk about that later. In fact, this is not a good time for any part of this conversation!"

"So he *is* marriage material?" Katrina asked.

"If he can get past the Boudreaux men," Maitlyn said with a mischievous laugh. "Did you see the video?"

"I'm done with all three of you!" Kamaya said, laughing. "Done and finished."

"Just come home at a decent hour, please," Maitlyn said. "I'm in labor. I predict this boy will make an appearance some time later tonight and it would be nice if his godmother were there to greet him."

"I thought I was his godmother?" Tarah said, pouting slightly.

"The next baby is yours," Maitlyn replied. "I promise."

"Can I name it, too?"

Katrina feigned a cough, clearing her throat. "Really, Tarah?"

"I'd pick good names! Petunia if it's a girl, to keep the flower thing going, and Zorba for a boy."

"No, you cannot name any child of mine!" Maitlyn exclaimed.

"I was teasing!" Tarah shot back. "But seriously, I actually like Iris or Lily for a baby girl. Then, since you and your husband are rolling with the letter Z for your boys, Zander or maybe Zahir?"

"I actually like Zahir!" Kamaya said matter-of-factly.

"I like them both," Katrina added. "And I *love* Lily for a girl. I might have to steal that one for myself."

"Are you pregnant again?" Kamaya asked.

There was a collective pause as they all waited for their eldest sister to respond.

"Hell, no! I was just having a moment!"

The laughter was gut deep and rich with emotion.

Katrina gasped as she caught her breath. "Maitlyn, I thought you said Zakar was going to be it? That you weren't having any more babies after this one?"

"I'm married to a man who's determined to keep me barefoot and pregnant, and I kind of like it. There's bound to be at least one more! Maybe even two."

Kamaya's excitement pierced her eyes. "Although I am thoroughly enjoying this conversation, I really must go. I think I hear Wesley calling my name." She tapped him with her foot, her eyebrows raised.

Wesley grinned. He cupped his hand over his mouth as Kamaya held the phone up. His voice was a loud, husky whisper as he pretended to yell. "Kamaya! Kamaya!"

She pulled the phone back to her ear. "See, I have to go. I promise I will be there and on time, Maitlyn! Just call me when you head to the hospital."

"One of us will definitely call you. We should all be landing before six," Katrina said.

"Is everyone flying in?" Kamaya questioned.

"I'm not," Tarah said. "I'm on call at the hospital, but Nicholas and I are coming in next weekend to meet our nephew. And Gianna is too far along in her pregnancy to make the trip so she and Donovan won't be able to make it. I think everyone else is, though."

"And bring my son's new Uncle Wesley with you. There's no time like the present for him to meet the family," Maitlyn said. "He's already covering for you, so that definitely makes him a keeper," she added as she mimicked him. *"Kamaya! Kamaya!"*

"Goodbye, Maitlyn!" Kamaya snapped.

Her sisters all laughed. "We love you, too!" the three-some chimed as Kamaya disconnected the call.

Wesley shot her a look. "Is everything okay?" he asked.

"Maitlyn's in labor!"

He shifted forward in the bed. "Do you need me to take you to her?"

She shook her head. "No, but I would appreciate a ride to the hospital later this evening, if you don't mind."

"Not at all. She's not there already?" His brow furrowed with confusion.

"Her babies take forever to come. Rose-Lynn had her in labor for seventeen hours. Zayn came in twelve. She refuses to take any drugs for the pain, so she never heads to the hospital until she absolutely has to."

"Wow!"

"Wow is right. I want drugs. I'm getting an epidural after the first cramp."

He laughed. "Duly noted. Marriage first. Drugs for baby."

She grinned "You catch on fast."

"I can actually walk and chew gum at the same time. I'm like a one-man carnival act!"

Kamaya laughed.

"So, I see that you and your sisters are really close. I only heard one side of the conversation and it sounded very entertaining."

"My sisters are my best friends. We share everything. Well, almost everything. But I'm sure I'm not the only one that has left out a detail or two about something."

"I'm thinking ownership of a multi-million-dollar adult entertainment operation is more than a detail."

"It depends on your perspective," Kamaya said, as she rolled her eyes.

Wesley leaned back against the pillows, returning to his newspaper.

"Do you think I'm fast?" she asked, suddenly curious.

Wesley peered at her over his paper. He laughed. "Fast *and* hot tailed, is what my mother would say."

"So what does that make you? Because I didn't sleep with myself." There was the faintest hint of attitude in her tone.

He reached for her, pulling her onto his lap. He wrapped her in a deep bear hug. "That, beautify lady, makes me crazy about you."

"Good answer," Kamaya said as she kissed him. "I refuse to be labeled a slut just because I enjoy getting mine, when you would get a pat on the back and a notch on your boy's card for doing the same thing."

"Are you feeling some kind of way about making love with me?" Wesley brushed a loose curl out of her face.

She pondered his question for a quick minute. "Yeah," she said finally. "I'm feeling like the luckiest damn woman in the whole wide world!"

Chapter 10

The waiting room of the family birthing center at Touro Infirmary looked like a Boudreaux family reunion. Kamaya's parents, her siblings and their spouses were all waiting anxiously for news about Maitlyn and her baby.

Kamaya's twin was the first to key in on her and the man she was holding hands with when she entered the room. Kendrick eyed them both as she guided Wesley to where her parents sat, introducing them to each other. Kamaya felt his gaze narrowing as he took in Wesley's imposing stance.

"Who's that with my Yaya?" he asked, moving to where Katrina was sitting with his wife, Vanessa, and his sisters-in-law, Phaedra and Dahlia.

"That's Kamaya's new *boo*," Katrina whispered back. "I think Maitlyn's the only one who's met him, but his name is Wesley."

"My, my, my!" Vanessa muttered. "Ain't he all GQ!" she exclaimed, exchanging a look with the other woman.

Phaedra laughed. "Yes, yes, yes!" she said under her breath.

Dahlia echoed the sentiment. "I'd like to interview him for one of my movies. He is too sweet!"

Kendrick tossed the women a look and they all burst out laughing a second time. He shook his head.

"What's so funny?" Kamaya questioned, moving to where they all sat, having overheard every part of their *secret* conversation.

"Your brother," Vanessa teased. She waved at Wesley. "Hi!"

Kendrick gave Wesley the once-over, his eyes skipping from his head to his feet and back. "Kendrick Boudreaux, Kamaya's twin, and you are?"

Wesley smiled. "Wesley Walters, Kamaya's boyfriend. It's a pleasure to meet you."

"Boyfriend?" Kendrick cut an eye at Wesley, and then his sister and back.

Kamaya's eyes skipped toward the ceiling, her brow furrowing in annoyance. "Don't start, Kendrick."

"What? I didn't say anything, but since you brought it up, I've never known you to date *boys*." Kendrick's gaze was locked on Wesley's face.

Kamaya slammed her fist into her brother's arm. "That was so not cool, Kendrick!"

Wesley chuckled. "It's all good. He's just being protective."

"He's being an ass!" Kamaya griped.

Kendrick shrugged, still rubbing at the rising bruise where she had just punched him.

"Wesley, this is Kendrick's wife, Vanessa, and my

sister-in-law, Dahlia. Dahlia is married to my brother Guy. And this is Phaedra. She's Mason's wife."

Wesley shook hands with all the women. "It's nice to meet you," he said. "I'm a big fan of your work, Ms. Morrow. I think your movie *Passionate* was one of my all-time favorites."

Dahlia smiled. "Thank you."

Zakaria Sayed suddenly rushed into the room. Moving behind Kamaya, his hands dropped against her shoulders. "Just the woman I was looking for!"

"Hey Zak! Where's Maitlyn?"

"They just got her settled in the delivery room."

"Zakaria, this is Wesley. Wesley, this is Maitlyn's husband, Zakaria Sayed."

The two men exchanged a head nod.

"It's a pleasure to meet you, Wesley," Zak said. "My wife spoke very highly of you."

"Maitlyn is very kind. I enjoyed talking with her."

Zak tapped Kamaya's shoulders. "Maitlyn sent me to get you. She said you *have* to be there. It's optional for the rest of you girls."

Katherine Boudreaux interjected from her seat across the room. "All us girls are going in. Dr. Bailey knows he can't keep us from seeing that baby come into the world." The woman stood up, joining the small group where they stood. "You boys make yourselves comfortable. It might be a minute."

The matriarch turned her attention to her son. "Kendrick, introduce Kamaya's *man* friend to the rest of the family. And act like you've had some home training, please. You should be excited that your sister has finally brought someone around for us to meet."

Kendrick shot his twin a look, her grin pulling

wide and full across her face. He shook his head as he wrapped his arm around Kamaya's shoulder and leaned to kiss her forehead. He extended his arm in Wesley's direction. There was a moment of hesitation and then the two shook hands.

Katherine looped her arm through Zakaria's. "Let's go welcome my new grandbaby!" she said.

The two led the way, Kamaya and the other female members of the family following them eagerly.

Kendrick turned toward Wesley. He opened his mouth to speak, but Senior suddenly moved between them.

"So, Wesley, what is it you do?" the older man asked, his arms crossed over his chest.

Wesley took a deep breath. "I have a number of real estate investments, sir, and most recently I purchased a nightclub that I'm managing."

"The bar business never grows old," Senior responded. "Folks are always looking for a good time. Did you meet my son Mason?"

Mason stepped up to shake Wesley's hand. "You actually look familiar to me. Have we met before?"

Wesley nodded. "Very briefly. You spoke at a business conference hosted by the 100 Black Men of Metro New Orleans a few years ago."

Mason paused, a moment of reflection passing as he thought back. "You came up to me and asked about franchises."

"I did," Wesley said, impressed that he remembered. "I wanted to know your opinion of them relative to their investment potential."

"Did you pursue them further?"

"I did. I actually acquired my first one a few months ago."

"Well, it's nice to see you again. Kamaya threw you right into the fire without a life vest, didn't she?" He chuckled warmly.

Wesley laughed. "I hope she trusts that I can handle myself."

"I'd hate to see you if you can't," another of Kamaya's brothers interjected, moving to join the conversation. "Kamaya will cut a brother loose in a heartbeat if he doesn't measure up." He greeted Wesley warmly. "I'm Darryl Boudreaux. Welcome to the madhouse!"

"You're the engineer married to the architect, right?" Wesley asked.

Darryl nodded. "That would be me!"

"And Kamaya can be cold," Mason confirmed, as he gestured for them all to take a seat.

"Hell, all of these women can be cold!" their brother Guy tossed in.

Senior laughed. "I can't speak for the women you boys married, but when it comes to your sisters, that's all your mama. They took right after her!"

"And you!" Mason exclaimed. "From day one you taught them all to not take any crap from anyone. Every one of them listened and learned."

"A little too well, if you ask me," Kendrick muttered. He cut an eye at Wesley then shifted his gaze away.

Senior shifted forward in his seat, his hands folded together in front of him. "So, young man, how long have you and my daughter known one another?"

Wesley took a deep breath, a wave of anxiety blowing over him as all the Boudreaux men leaned forward, waiting for him to respond. "Kamaya's business partner, Paxton, introduced us about a month ago."

"So this thing between you is new?" Senior commented.

"Yes, sir!" Wesley nodded. "We're getting to know each other and have just been enjoying each other's company."

The older man's head moved up and down. "Where are you originally from? You don't sound like you have roots here in New Orleans."

"I don't, sir. I was born and raised in Alabama."

"Did your parents raise you in the church?"

Wesley smiled. "Yes, sir. Baptist born and bred. Both are in worship service every Sunday like clockwork."

The patriarch nodded, his own grin widening. "Your father's a better man than I am. I get my hallelujahs in at least once a month, but I can't commit to Mass every Sunday! I look forward to meeting him."

Light laughter filled the room. For another thirty minutes the men bantered back and forth. Wesley fielded a host of questions. He was comfortable and enjoying the camaraderie. For the most part Kamaya's brothers were welcoming, although Kendrick wasn't warming up to Wesley as fast as the others.

"I'm going on a coffee run," Kendrick said. "Everyone want one?" After fielding a round of orders he turned to Wesley. "Why don't you come give me a hand, *champ*?"

Wesley nodded. "Sure thing, *sport*!"

Senior laughed out loud, and the others chuckled as they eyed the two men, waiting to see who might jump first.

Neither spoke as they headed down the hall to the

hospital elevators. Once inside, Kendrick looked Wesley up and down one more time. "You know I'm going to run a background check on you, right? I'm just putting it out there. I don't want you to be surprised if I find anything my sister needs to know because I will make sure she hears it."

Wesley laughed. "Sorry to disappoint you, but your sister Maitlyn has already beaten you to it. I'm sure she, or Kamaya, will be able to get you up to speed."

There was a moment's pause as Kendrick stood staring at him. "What are your intentions with my twin?" he finally asked.

Wesley stared back. "For now," he said, "I just want to make her as happy as I possibly can."

The two stood as if they'd come to an impasse. The elevators opened at the cafeteria floor. Kendrick stepped out first. "Hurt my sister and I will hurt you," he said, shooting Wesley a look over his shoulder.

Wesley smiled as he followed after the man. "And what if your sister hurts me?"

"You seem like a pretty tough guy. You'll get over it. They all do. And when that happens, I'll even buy you a beer to take the sting off." There was a smirk across his face.

Wesley nodded. "Is she really that rough on the men she dates?"

Kendrick grinned. "Notoriously! Kamaya has chewed up and spit out the best of the best." He slapped Wesley across the back. "But look at it this way. You're in good company!"

Zakar Sayed pushed his way into the world kicking and screaming. He was seven pounds, four ounces, and loud, crying at the top of his little lungs. Kamaya cradled the newborn infant in her arms, rocking him gently back and forth.

"What's wrong with him?" she asked, tossing her mother a panicked look.

Katherine laughed. "Not a thing! Give him back to his mother. He's having separation anxiety. Poor soul gets ripped out of the womb and then everyone wants to pass him around like a football. He just wants to get back to his mommy's body heat and that booby juice."

"Well, he's welcome to it," Kamaya said, as she eased her new godchild into his mother's arms.

Maitlyn smiled, cooing at her new son softly. "Hey, sweet baby! How's mama's baby boy?"

"My son is perfect!" Zakaria exclaimed, his grin canyon wide, his chest pushed forward with pride. Maitlyn tilted her head to kiss his lips. "Absolutely perfect," he repeated.

There was a knock on the hospital room door. Senior pushed it open slightly and poked his head inside. "Y'all decent in here?" he asked.

"Come meet your new grandson," Katherine commanded.

The room was suddenly flooded with family, all the men joining in the celebration.

"Lookie here, lookie here," the old man said as he moved to the bedside. Senior kissed his daughter's cheek as he leaned to peer at the infant in her arms. Baby Zakar had finally settled down, slumbering comfortably. Senior shook Zakaria's hand. "Good job! He's a fine boy!"

Zak nodded his appreciation as he basked in the good wishes, moving around the room to pass out cigars.

From where she stood by the window, Kamaya caught Wesley's eye. The man was hanging back nervously.

"You're still standing, I see!" she said, as she eyed him with a raised brow.

Wesley nodded, her bright expression sending his spirit sky high.

Maitlyn looked from him, to her sister, then exchanged a knowing look with her mother.

Katherine chuckled. "Wesley, surviving my sons is no big deal. Your challenge is going to be that daughter of mine."

Wesley laughed. "So I've heard."

Kamaya rolled her eyes. "I am not that bad!"

Her siblings all laughed, heads shaking from side to side.

Senior crossed to where Kamaya stood and wrapped her in a warm embrace. "Hang in there, son! We want to see Kamaya right where her sister Maitlyn is someday."

"Senior!"

"Don't Senior me!" he answered, kissing her cheek. "We kind of like this one."

Kamaya tossed up her hands. She shook her head, her gaze locking with Wesley's. "Please, don't pay any of them any attention," she said.

Wesley laughed. "Too late. Now I'm officially scared," he responded as he winked at her.

Kamaya eased her way to where he stood, stepping into his arms as she hugged him around the waist. "You should be!"

Chapter 11

Weeks later Kamaya and Wesley had settled into a comfortable routine with each other. When they weren't working they divided their time between his home, her home and the boat. On weekends they disappeared to wherever their mood moved them, and any time they spent together was all about having a good time.

Wesley had insisted on a soft opening for The Wet Bar, wanting to test the club's operations to diagnose and correct any problems they might have had without enduring the scrutiny that would come with the grand opening. The nominal fanfare that had come had been more than enough to kick start the business. Paired with the entertainment feature that had been filmed for the local news station, shining a spotlight on the club and the dancers, it took no time at all before they were the talk of the town. Since then, friends had been telling friends and the enthusiastic crowds were growing steadily. Wesley had a winning formula on his hands and Kamaya couldn't begrudge him his due. What both had thought to be a sure moneymaker was turning out to be so much more.

Kamaya reviewed the quarterly numbers for all of her companies. Business was going exceptionally well and each day that they were able to keep her secret, and Wesley's, was a good day. She was ready to do a happy dance over how well things seemed to be working out for the two of them.

Wesley had finally met all of her family and he seemed to enjoy hanging out with her brothers. Even he and Kendrick looked like they were going to be good buddies. His parents were scheduled to visit soon, and Kamaya was actually looking forward to spending time with them. She and Wesley's mother had spoken on the telephone a few times and the similarities to her mother were striking. Mrs. Walters was exceptionally kind and she made Kamaya feel comfortable. Even her teasing about wanting grandchildren had been good-natured, moving them both to giggle.

Kamaya loved that she and Wesley laughed so much. He didn't take himself so seriously, and he took much joy in making her laugh at herself. When they weren't together they talked incessantly on the phone, both having an opinion about everything under the sun. Wesley often played devil's advocate, which made for some interesting debates.

Being with him was easy. He allowed her to be herself and there was never a need for pretenses. He still liked her even when she regularly pushed his buttons for a reaction. No man had ever allowed her such freedom and as they continued to explore their relationship she had come to trust that he would never try to change who she was.

They both loved food; down-home soul cooking was his favorite, and anything Kamaya didn't have to cook was hers. The two bonded over their mutual interest in reggae music, dislike of reality television, penchant for English football and their aversion to cold weather. They discovered they had more in common than not, and the beauty of that made their growing friendship intense and eternal.

Kamaya slid the financial spreadsheets back into their manila folder. She was past ready to head home when Paxton suddenly burst into her office. He was flustered and out of breath, and looked like he'd slept in his favorite designer suit.

"Hey, what's wrong with you?" she asked, her gaze narrowed.

Her friend shook his head. "I've been calling you all weekend. You didn't pick up."

"I was away."

"With who? Where did you go?" He eyed her with a raised brow, curiosity seeping from his stare.

"Why are you acting so damn weird, Paxton? What's wrong?" She rose from her seat and moved to stand in front of her desk. Her arms were crossed over her chest, her brow creased with concern.

"Laney's husband died."

"No!" she exclaimed. "What happened?"

Paxton shook his head, suddenly more flustered than when he'd arrived.

Kamaya's eyes widened. "Oh, my God! She killed her husband?"

He shook his head. "Laney did not kill her husband. Why do you always do that?"

"Do what?"

"Expect the worst from her."

"Uh, because she's like the bubonic plague in a designer dress and high heels. Just because you put lipstick on a pig doesn't mean it isn't still a pig!"

"Really, Kamaya?"

"Paxton, the woman is toxic. She treats you like crap. Everything is always about her. She doesn't love you. Hell, she barely even cares about you."

He rolled his eyes. "You're just bitter."

Kamaya bristled. "On that note, you have a good night."

"I needed your help! I thought you were my friend."

"I am your friend and I'm not about to sugarcoat anything for you. You, of all people, know how this works. You either take me as I am or you don't."

"That doesn't give you license to be so damn mean!"

"I'm not being mean. I'm being honest and I can't help it if the truth hurts."

"Sometimes you can be a little *too* honest."

"Whatever!"

"I need a favor. The police might call and ask if you know where I was…"

Kamaya gasped. She took a step backward. "Please do not tell me *you* killed her husband."

The look Paxton gave her was priceless, annoyance a bright shade of red that made him look like he was about to explode. His voice cracked as he admonished her. "Of course not! He died in a car accident. He got hit in the rear and pushed into oncoming traffic. A tractor trailer carrying cows hit him broadside."

"Cows? Really?"

"Okay, maybe not cows but it was some kind of delivery truck. It could have been goats or sheep for all I know. I just know it was some kind of farm animal."

Kamaya stifled a laugh and rolled her eyes before settling her gaze back on him. "Why would the police need to confirm your whereabouts?"

"His children are claiming someone tampered with his brakes."

"Did they?"

"How would I know? I didn't do it!"

"So, where were you this weekend?"

"If anyone asks I was here, working."

"But where were you?" Kamaya persisted.

"Laney and I flew to Vegas for the weekend. We were shacked up at the Mirage."

"Like any good investigator won't find that out," she said sarcastically.

"We just don't want her husband's kids to find out. They're vowing to challenge his will if he left her more than a dime. They had an infidelity clause in their prenup."

"So, she had an infidelity clause in her prenuptial agreement and she still cheated on her husband with you?"

Paxton shrugged, his eyes skating everywhere but toward her.

Kamaya gave him a blank stare. Her friend had truly slumped to a whole new low. She shook her head.

"So you'll cover for me?"

"If anyone asks I'll tell them you *said* you were here working, but since I was out of town I can neither confirm nor deny."

"I knew you wouldn't have my back. It's a good thing I don't need your help."

"You should have known that I'm not doing time for you and that black widow. People have gone to jail for far less. I'm not going out like that."

"Remind me to never use you for an alibi if I ever do kill someone!"

"Don't kill anyone. Unless it's Laney. Then you can call me to bring you a shovel and new rose bush. I'll even pick up fertilizer on my way there."

"You are so evil!" Paxton brushed his blond locks out of his eyes. "Seriously, her old man died and the past few days have been hell. I called because I just needed to vent and you're one of the only people who will let me. So, tell me again where you were?"

"I didn't tell you where I was the first time."

"Yes, you did!"

"No, I didn't. I told you I was away. That's all I said."

"So where were you?"

Kamaya shook her head.

"Then tell me who you were with?"

"A friend."

"Do I know this friend?"

"You know that I never tell you my personal business. You know this, and yet you still ask."

"I have a moral responsibility. Besides, your brother pays me when I have information he can use."

"I'm done with you."

"Have dinner with me and Laney this week. She could really use a friend."

"Paxton, that woman and I will never be friends."

"Do it for me, please? And you can even bring my friend Wesley. We can make it a double date."

"Why would I bring Wesley?" she asked, noting the smug look on her friend's face.

Paxton laughed. "Rumor has it that you two are an item now. If I were a betting man, I'd bet that you were playing hide the salami with him all weekend."

She shook her head. "Who the hell have you been talking to?"

He shrugged. "Kendrick called me. Your brother had some concerns."

"Aargh!" Kamaya screamed. "I swear, I'm killing him and then I'm killing you!"

Paxton laughed. "Do you need an alibi?"

Kamaya flipped him off as she moved back behind her desk, dropping into her seat.

"So vent. Because you look like you've had a really rough time."

She and her pal sat staring at each other, amusement dancing between them. The banter was easy and teasing as they caught up, Paxton filling her in on his nightmare of a weekend. Kamaya couldn't help but think it was just another one of his sad sob stories starring the love of his life. But for the first time she actually felt sorry for him, wishing that he would one day see what she saw and find someone who genuinely loved and cared for him. But as he spoke, the details of his Laney tribulations sounded like a Shakespearean drama with no happy ending in sight.

Her mood shifted, the energy in the room turning serious. "You know I love you, right?"

Paxton nodded. "Yeah, Kamaya, and I love you, too."

"Then you know that I only want the best for you."

He paused, eyeing her intently before he answered. "And you don't think Laney is best for me."

"I think that when it comes to matters of the heart we sometimes only see what we want to see. Your heart is completely caught up in this relationship, but you haven't allowed your head to get into the game."

He blew a heavy sigh. "And you think that's a bad thing?"

"I think you need to really think about where you want this relationship to go and consider why she might do some of the things she does. I don't want you to get hurt. That's all."

Paxton smiled. "You do care about me!"

"Don't get it twisted. You still owe me money. I'm protecting my investment."

His face twisted. "Cut a man some slack. It was just a small loan. I thought you would have forgiven that by now."

"We're talking about my money, not your bad habits."

They both laughed. She stood a second time. "I'm going home. I suggest you do the same."

He nodded. "I need to. I'm tired and it's starting to catch up with me."

"Well, I need you on top of your game tomorrow. Wesley has a site for his next franchise that he wants us to approve. Plus, we've got additional franchise inquiries coming in faster than we can field them. We have some decisions to make."

"I'm glad you two hooked up. He really is a great guy. If things work out, you might even want to consider bringing him in on the business as your partner."

"Where did that come from?" Kamaya questioned.

"I have new aspirations, Kamaya. Laney and I have been talking about starting something together and...

well…" He cut an uneasy eye at her. "Let's talk about it more tomorrow. I'm excited and I want you to be excited for me."

An uncomfortable pause settled over them. It rose thick and full, a force field of weight that wouldn't be moved easily. Kamaya slowly nodded her head, and as Paxton turned, his hand on the doorknob, something her brother Mason had told her when she'd first started out in business rang loudly in her head. *You can't soar with eagles if you're out hootin' with the owls.*

"You have a good night," Paxton said, as he made his exit, tossing her one last glance over his shoulder.

As the door closed and his footsteps faded off in the distance, Kamaya finally responded softly. "I'm going to miss you," she whispered.

"He does see it," Wesley was saying as he shifted his cell phone from one ear to the other. "But he loves her. So if he's willing to tolerate her behavior, why does it bother you so much?"

"Because he's my friend," Kamaya answered. "And he deserves so much better!"

Wesley could hear the frustration in her voice. She'd called him ranting about Paxton as she'd pulled out of the parking lot of her office, heading in the direction of her home. Even Wesley had agreed that her best friend's final comments had sounded foreboding, like more bad news was definitely coming her way.

"He's leaving the business. I can feel it. Somehow that witch has convinced him to go into business with her. I can't believe he's even considering it!"

Wesley sighed. "So what if he does leave? Is it going to be a problem if you have to buy out his interest?"

"No. He only owns thirty percent of the business and he owes me money. I have more than enough cash on hand if he's owed a payout. That's not a problem at all."

Wesley nodded into his receiver. "I know you want to help him, Kamaya, but you can't help a man who's not ready to help himself. Clearly, whatever is going on with him and his woman is important to him. If he's not ready to let that go, there's absolutely nothing you can do to change his mind."

"It just doesn't make sense to me."

"Let me tell you about an old friend of mine."

"Is this a friend I'm going to meet?"

"Probably," he said. "At some point I'm sure I'll get an opportunity to introduce the two of you." He could hear her car engine turn off. "You home?

"I am. I'm going to take you off speaker while I get into the house. Hold on a minute for me."

"Just be careful," he said, as she went quiet. There was an extended moment of bags rustling and doors slamming before she spoke again.

"Sorry, baby. So, tell me about your friend," Kamaya said, as she moved into the interior of her house and dropped down onto the living room sofa.

"My friend Jack married his childhood sweetheart, Marcy. He has loved Marcy since they were both twelve years old. But Marcy never loved Jack the same way. They had only been married a few months when he started complaining about her flirting with other men, and then the flirting turned to cheating. Marcy would disappear for days at a time, come home, beg Jack to forgive her and he would. Years go by, Marcy now has five kids and Jack is not the father of any one of them."

"Oh, hell no! And he didn't leave her?"

"No. Each and every time she'd apologize and talk her way back into his head. We would all give him advice, offer him support, everything, but Marcy had that kind of hold on him."

"That's a shame!"

"It is. Anyway, about three years ago Marcy was arrested for check fraud. And she was arrested with some man who said he was her boyfriend. Jack said he was done. Marcy got some jail time and Jack filed for divorce. Last year, Marcy got out of prison and before you know it she had moved back in with Jack. He said it was only temporary but she's still there, still running his life, still doing her dirt and he just can't let her go."

"That's just crazy! He should have kicked Marcy to the curb!"

"I think so, but since I'm not in his shoes and I don't know what goes on behind his closed doors, there's nothing I can do but be there to support him when things go bad. I know in my heart of hearts that things will eventually go bad. All you can do is let Paxton know that you'll be here for him if he needs you when things go bad for him. And if by chance the two of them actually make things work, then you still just need to be the friend he knows he can depend on."

Kamaya blew a soft sigh. "Be honest. Does my friendship with Paxton bother you?"

"It bothers me that you are stressed about him. And it bothers me because there's nothing that I can do to take that stress from you."

Her voice dropped an octave. "Oh, there's something you can do," she said, her sultry tone moving him to smile. "In fact, if I think about it, I'm sure there are a few things that I can come up with for you to do."

"Just give me a list, baby!"

"Thank you," Kamaya said, her voice a loud whisper.

"For what?"

"For letting me vent. I appreciate that I can talk to you about anything and you don't think I'm crazy when I go off on one of my rants."

"Well, I don't know about all that, now!" he said teasingly. "You might be a little bit crazy!"

Kamaya laughed. "Actually, I might be a lot crazy! Consider yourself warned!"

Their conversation continued for another good hour. When they finally hung up, promising to talk again in the early morning hours, both were wishing they'd made plans to spend the night together. Her missing him was only outdone by his missing her. Wesley dialed her right back.

"Hey! What's wrong?" Kamaya asked, answering on the first ring.

"I can't sleep."

Kamaya laughed. "You haven't tried!"

"I don't need to. You're not here so I know I'm going to toss and turn for the next few hours."

She smiled. "I miss you, too."

"Are you coming here or am I coming there?"

Kamaya laughed. "What are you wearing?"

"I still have on my suit. I was just about to get out of my clothes."

"I'm only wearing my bra and panties."

Wesley laughed. "I'm on my way!"

Hours later Wesley whispered her name, easing behind her as she allowed her body to melt into his. Her back rested against his broad chest, her buttocks cradled neatly into the curve of his crotch. His fingers trailed a line of heat down the length of her arm and torso, and then he snaked his hand down between her legs, the teasing gesture moving her to moan.

Making love to Wesley was like getting the cherry off some very sweet cake. Each and every time they were together felt like the first time, his touch stirring something deep inside of her spirit. Falling asleep in any man's arms wasn't something Kamaya had ever needed. She'd actually refused herself the luxury. But resting in Wesley's arms was everything, the intensity of being near him fueling something she hadn't even known she wanted.

And she wanted Wesley. She wanted him with every fiber of her being. She missed him when they were apart, and for the first time she couldn't imagine her life without him there.

She turned, twisting against the mattress until she could press her face beneath the curve of his chin, pressing a damp kiss against his skin. Her hands skated around his torso as she hugged him close, and he pulled her tight against his chest. She took a deep inhale of air, the decadent scent of his cologne like the sweetest balm.

He kissed her forehead and then her lips. "You good?" he whispered softly, that thick Southern drawl of his making her smile.

She shook her head, her mouth lifting in the easiest bend. "No!"

His eyes opened as he stared down at her. "What's wrong, baby?"

Kamaya reached her hand between them, wrapping her fingers around his male member. "I'm needy," she whispered. "Very needy."

Wesley laughed, his organ twitching against her palm. He leaned to kiss her lips a second time.

"What do you want?" he asked, his voice a low, husky whisper.

"No," she said, whispering back. "It's a need!" she gushed.

He laughed again. "You need me?"

"I do. I need you and I don't ever want to lose you." The words spilled past her lips before she could catch them. Her eyes closed for a brief second as she tightened the hug she had around him.

"I'm not going anywhere," Wesley said softly. "You're going to have a hard time getting rid of me." He kissed her forehead, his lips fluttering lightly against her skin.

"Good, because I really like what we have."

"What exactly do we have, Kamaya? I know you have an aversion to labeling your relationships, but what is going on with us?"

There was a moment of pause as the couple lay side by side, staring at each other. Kamaya shrugged her shoulders ever so slightly. "I just know that I don't want to lose us. Isn't that enough?"

"That can be taken a number of ways."

"How do you want to take it?"

"I'd like to think that you love me, and because you love me you want to spend the rest of your life with me. In fact, you love me so much that you would marry me and have my children."

"Love? Isn't that rushing things a bit?"

"Maybe, but you can't stop the heart from having what it wants. You love me."

"And how do you know that's how I feel?"

"Because I love you more than anything else in this world. I love you and I want to spend the rest of my life with you. I love you, Kamaya Boudreaux."

She pressed her palm to his cheek and lifted her lips to his, kissing him gently. "So, are you interested in doing business with me?" she asked. "I'm going to need a partner."

He chuckled softly. "Outline the details in our pre-nup and I'll consider it."

"I don't believe in prenups," she said matter-of-factly.

His brows lifted in surprise. "You, the contract queen of business dos and don'ts, don't believe in prenups?"

"A prenup says I don't trust you. And if I love you, then I trust you with my life."

He reflected on her comments for a brief moment. He cupped his hand beneath her chin and lifted her eyes to his. "Do you trust me, Kamaya?"

She smiled sweetly. "With my life."

Chapter 12

Waking next to Wesley was a wonderful way to start each new day. Without verbalizing what they were doing, Kamaya and Wesley had managed to move in with each other, one week in his space, the next in hers. It worked for them, and when it didn't, neither had any problem fixing it so that it did. But when Kamaya found herself being questioned about their relationship, what was easy and comfortable suddenly wasn't.

"I like him, Kamaya. Your daddy and I both do, but you know how we feel about you shacking up with any man."

The young woman winced. "Wesley and I are not *shacking up*. We…well…it's complicated."

Her mother eyed her with a raised brow. "I may have been born at night, Kamaya, but I wasn't born last night. When he's not at your house, you're at his. You sleep together every night. That's shacking up."

"We don't always sleep," Kamaya mumbled under her breath.

Maitlyn laughed, rocking her infant son against her shoulder.

Katherine shot her daughters a look. "I heard that. Your father and I have told you about that smart mouth of yours. You are not too old!"

Tarah laughed. "Finally! Someone else is getting all the heat."

Katherine pointed her finger. "I'm sure your turn is coming. You both need to take some pointers from Maitlyn and Katrina."

Katrina brushed the back of her fingers against her shoulder. She winked at Maitlyn "Yes, you two should take pointers from us. We're good girls!"

Kamaya rolled her eyes. "Didn't you have a baby before you married that husband of yours?

Tarah nodded. "You did do that!"

"Really!" Katrina retorted. You're going to call me out like that?"

Kamaya continued. "I was just pointing out that you two weren't *that* good! Maitlyn had vacation sex with a man she'd only known for a few hours."

Maitlyn laughed. "Yes, I did, and now that man and I are married with three kids. What's your point?"

"When you think about it," Tarah interjected. "I've been a really good girl in comparison to the rest of you heathens!"

"And you were the one we were most worried about," Katherine added. She leaned to kiss her daughter's forehead. "Sure did surprise me and your daddy!"

A round of laughter rang heartily around the room.

Kamaya shook her head. "So, what are we doing?" she questioned.

It was a milestone birthday for Katherine, her seventy-fifth, and all of her children and grandchildren were flying in to celebrate. Kamaya and her sisters had arrived first, plotting an all-girls celebration for the evening before the kickoff of the family festivities that were scheduled for Sunday afternoon after Mass.

"Maitlyn made reservations for us at GW Fins and then we're going clubbing!"

"Clubbing?" Katherine exclaimed. "I think I'm just a little too old for clubbing!"

"You will never be too old for a good time," Maitlyn said. "There's a new dance club called The Wet Bar that everyone is raving about. It caters to women and they tell me the men who dance there are to die for!"

Heat suddenly flooded Kamaya's face, and her cheeks flushed with color. "The Wet Bar?"

"It already sounds sinful!" Katherine said with a deep chuckle.

Katrina laughed. "Please tell me this isn't what I think it is!"

"It is!" Tarah exclaimed. "Male strippers!"

"Oh, I know you have lost your mind!" Katherine exclaimed. "Your father will have a fit!"

"That's why we're not telling him," Katrina said, tossing a quick look over her shoulder toward the door. "We're not telling any of the men. Not until we get back, anyway."

"Maybe we shouldn't…" Kamaya started.

Maitlyn waved a dismissive hand. "We're going and we're going to have a great time. And if it is too much, we can always leave and go get a drink at your boyfriend's bar."

The last of the color in Kamaya's face drained into the wine she gulped suddenly. Things had gone from bad to worse.

Katherine giggled. "Lord, have mercy! What time do I need to be ready?"

Despite her best efforts, Kamaya hadn't been able to convince her family that going to a male strip club was not a good idea. She had hoped that her mother would have declared a moratorium on the idea, but Katherine actually seemed to be looking forward to the prospect. As they were finishing their desserts, Kamaya gave it one last try.

"What about your work to stamp out sexual exploitation? Won't they have to revoke your cause card if you're patronizing strippers?" Kamaya questioned. She shot a look at her sisters before resting her gaze on their matriarch.

Katherine paused for a moment to reflect on the question. "Are these men being forced to work in this industry."

"No!" Tarah exclaimed, shooting Kamaya an agitated look.

"Are they being paid a fair wage for what they're doing?" Katherine asked.

"From what I know," Maitlyn said, "they're being paid very well. And their tips are substantial."

"A lot of horny women making it rain!" Tarah laughed.

Katherine cut her eyes at her youngest daughter before she continued. "I don't have enough information about the business or the men who are working there to form an opinion. But if I have any concerns, I have no problem contacting the owner and doing what might be needed to help any employee, male or female."

Kamaya took another gulp of wine. "So, you're okay with men shaking their assets for profit but you're opposed to women doing the same thing? Isn't that a little sexist?"

"What I am opposed to, Kamaya, is adults who manipulate and take advantage of children and young people who are not legally able to make decisions for themselves. Those who lack the maturity and emotional capability to understand that they are being taken advantage of. Individuals who become caught up in the sex trade and feel trapped in situations not of their making. I'm opposed to anyone, male or female, being forced to use their bodies for financial gain when the decision to do so wasn't made by them. I will rally against that all day, every day!

"I am *not* opposed to adults who fully understand the significance and consequences of their actions opting to make their living in that manner. I don't know the ages of these men, but I would be concerned if I thought that they weren't aware of the pitfalls of this lifestyle or if I got the sense that they were being taken advantage of."

"There are pitfalls?" Tarah asked.

Her mother nodded. "Of course! Most strippers are hired as independent contractors, not as full-time employees. They have to deal with job insecurity, unstable pay and no health benefits. Most have to pay fees to the club for renting their stage. Then, of course, there is the stigma associated with exotic dancing. There are definitely pitfalls. A child doesn't understand that. Most adults do."

"Well, I think we should just go to a movie or something," Kamaya muttered.

"Why does it sound like you don't want your mother to find out you're a freak, Kamaya?" Tarah asked, her brows raised as she stared at her sister.

Katrina and Maitlyn both laughed. Kamaya cut her eyes at the trio, not at all amused.

Katherine laughed along with Kayama. "Way too late for that!" she proclaimed. "Way too late!"

After excusing herself to use the restroom, Kamaya tried for the umpteenth time to call Wesley. When it went right to voice mail she shot him another text message, frustrated that she still hadn't heard back from him.

"Answer the phone," she muttered as she paced in front of the line of sinks. "Please, answer the phone!"

She took a deep breath, trying to decide how to keep her mother and siblings from discovering Wesley's connection to the salacious business. They all knew he owned a nightclub. For whatever reason, most of her family thought it was a quiet jazz joint on the other side of town. She had never bothered to correct their confusion and she'd insisted he roll with it, as well. She suddenly imagined it all blowing up in her face when they walked in and he stood there, front and center, doling out orders.

"Think, think, think!" she muttered again as she paced a few minutes more.

She'd typed one last text message and was about to

push the Send button when Tarah and Katrina burst into the room.

"What's taking you?" Tarah said, eyeing her curiously.

"Yeah, what are you up to?" Katrina asked. "Because you're up to something."

"I am not!"

"I bet she's sleeping with one of the dancers!" Tarah suddenly exclaimed. "You're sleeping with one of the dancers and cheating on Wesley!"

"I am not!" Kamaya snapped.

"Then one of them is an ex. Is that it?" Tarah persisted.

Kamaya shook her head. "You still have a very vivid imagination, I see!"

Katrina laughed. "I'm betting it's an ex, too! And I wouldn't be surprised if he still has the hots for you!"

Kamaya grinned. She pushed the Send arrow on her screen then dropped the device into her purse. "Neither one of you knows what the hell you're talking about!"

Wesley was pacing back and forth, his anxiety rising tenfold. He cussed, noting the nonexistent battery level on his cell phone.

Bryan sat in his seat, his feet resting nonchalantly atop the desk. "So, what are we going to do?" he asked.

Wesley shot him a look. "Explain to me again why none of my dancers have punched in?"

Bryan blew an exasperated sigh. "Victor and Trey were offered a nice side job to dance for some private women's club in Shreveport. It was some lunch thing to honor the club's president. They needed extra dancers, so they shared the joy with the other guys. Trey rented a bus and they all drove up this morning. They're on their way back, but apparently the bus is giving them some trouble. They had to call AAA for a tow and get a new ride. They're stuck on the side of the road waiting to be picked up. They'll be here, but they're going to be a little late."

"Who's on call that we can get here in the next hour?"

"Goldberg is down in the bayou somewhere, at his little sister's wedding reception. He said he can be on the road and here by eleven-thirty."

"Which puts him here at midnight, too."

"Or sooner. With any luck."

"How the hell does something like this happen?" Wesley asked, exasperation seeping through each word.

"We need to make sure we put some restrictions on the outside work they can take. It seemed fine at the time, and when they ran it by me I didn't think it would be a problem. They had an enthusiastic audience, which I thought would be great advertisement for us."

Wesley blew a heavy breath, his head moving from side to side. "So, who do we have here now that's ready to dance, besides you?

"The new kid. He calls himself Titus Blow."

Wesley tossed a look in his friend's direction, displeasure racing across his face.

Bryan shrugged his broad shoulders. "We were working on that. He didn't like any of my suggestions, and since I wasn't planning on putting him out on the floor for at least another week or two it wasn't an issue."

"Well, now it's an issue. Can he at least dance?"

"Oh, he can dance! He's got mad skills, and I don't see any problems with him soloing. It was the group routines he hasn't been able to get a handle on."

"Okay, so we have a show that's supposed to start at ten o'clock. And we only have two dancers, maybe three, until the rest of the guys get here at midnight. And that's if they can even get here then."

"Actually, we have *four* dancers." Bryan's expression was smug as he dropped his legs to the floor and shifted forward in the seat. He folded his hands together against the desk top, his eyebrows raised as he stared at his friend.

"Who else…?" Wesley started.

Bryan's eyebrows rose even higher, his head tilted slightly as his expression mutated into an air of self-satisfaction. He winked at his best friend.

"Oh, hell, no! That's not happening."

Bryan rose from his seat, moving to the one-way mirror that looked out over the club's main floor. It was close to showtime and the crowd was growing steadily. Women were filling the seats at a rapid pace, and both men knew that it would only be a matter of time before they were at capacity. From where the two stood looking out, there was no missing the energy in the room. The crowd was ready and excited for a good time. Disappointing them was not an option.

Bryan turned and gave him a look. "So if we open with Titus Blow, the kid can get them warmed up for the first thirty minutes. I can follow him and keep the ladies happy until eleven-fifteen or so. And then Deuce makes an unannounced, impromptu appearance and dances until midnight, or until Goldberg shows up, whichever comes first. Hopefully the boys will be back and in line by then. Unless you have a better plan?"

Wesley paused. "Yeah, I do. Introduce the kid as the Wild Child. We have a reputation to uphold."

* * *

Kamaya was actually surprised by the crowd. Wesley had been reporting excellent numbers, but seeing it firsthand put it in a whole other perspective. As they were led to a table, she stared at the oversized mirror that decorated the space. She knew Wesley's office was behind it, and although she could only see her reflection, from inside, she knew he could see them. She prayed that he had gotten her messages and was hiding there in the back until she could convince her family that male strippers were a waste of their good time.

When the waiter, a bare-chested clone of Gerard Butler came to take their drink orders, Kamaya ordered a one-and-one.

"Drink much?" Tarah asked, giggling as she ordered a Tequila Sunrise.

"What's a one-and-one?" Katrina asked.

"A shot of whisky with a beer chaser," Kamaya answered, her eyes still flitting back and forth across the room.

"Too much for me!" Maitlyn laughed. "I'll have a glass of Moscato, please!"

"Drink at all?" Tarah quipped.

"I'm still breast feeding. I pumped enough until tomorrow but I need my system clean by the time I need to put Zakar back on the breast tomorrow."

Kamaya shook her head. "I don't think our waiter wanted to hear all that," she said.

"TMI!" Tarah echoed, giggling softly.

"All of you drink too much!" Katherine said. She shook her head. "Young man, I'll have a white wine spritzer, please."

As he turned and headed toward the bar, they all followed him with their eyes, noting the exceptional fit of the young man's denim jeans.

Katrina cleared her throat. "Well, there's definitely no shortage of eye candy in here," she said.

A round of laughter swept between them.

Wesley was digging in his desk for a phone charger when Bryan moved back into the room. He had changed into his costume, wearing white leather chaps over a nylon penis sock, a matching studded vest and a high-crowned, wide-brimmed straw hat. He was oiled up, his white chocolate complexion glistening beneath the lights.

"You need to get dressed," Bryan said matter-of-factly. "Or undressed, depending how you want to look at it. And show some enthusiasm! Deuce is about to make a comeback!"

Wesley ignored him. "Have you heard from Vincent?"

Bryan nodded. "They're finally rolling. He said they're making good time but it's still going to be a minute. And Goldberg is on target to roll in about eleven-thirty so you shouldn't have to dance but for so long."

Wesley nodded. He cussed as he came up empty, the contents of the drawer strewn across the desktop. "Where is my damn phone charger?"

"One of the guys might have borrowed it. I would lend you mine but I didn't bring one."

"I need to call Kamaya. She needs to know why I need to dance tonight."

"Why? You need your girl's permission to get your hustle on?"

"My girl needs to know that this is an emergency

situation and when I told her that she would never have to worry about me dancing, that I didn't lie to her."

"Just call her from the office phone," Bryan said, pointing his index finger toward the desktop unit that sat on the corner of his desk.

"I did. She didn't pick up."

"Did you leave her a message?"

"That's really not the kind of message you want to leave your woman on a voice mail. I told her to call me back!" Frustration bellowed out of his mouth.

"Do I detect a hint of attitude in your tone?" Amusement danced over Bryan's face.

Wesley tossed the man a look, annoyance creasing his brow.

Bryan laughed. "She has you so whipped! You're in love with that woman!"

"Shut up!"

"Head over heels! You go, boy!"

"I swear, Bryan, if you don't leave me alone I'm going to bust you in the face!"

Before Bryan could respond there was a knock at the office door. He shot a look in Wesley's direction before he moved to the entrance. The newbie, a college student named Marquis Johnson, stood in the doorway. He had one hand wrapped around his dick and a *Hustler* magazine in the other.

"Bryan...hey... I'm sorry...but, well...nothing is working!" he stammered.

Bryan and Wesley exchanged a look and then both burst out laughing. Wesley shook his head. "Handle that, please!"

Bryan was still chuckling. "Come on stud. What's your girlfriend's name?"

"I don't have one," Marquis responded.

"So who was the last girl that gave you some?"

The young man grinned. "Cassandra, I think. And that girl was fine! Large breasts, small waist, and the widest hips and ass!"

"Let's work with that," Bryan said as the two disappeared down the hallway.

The house lights flickered on and off, and a roar of excitement rippled thought the room. The music, which had been low and seductive, was kicked up a notch, the DJ spinning an upbeat jam that had the crowd dancing in their seats.

Tarah tossed her arms in the air and screamed her excitement with the other women. The energy was infectious and Kamaya laughed, joining in the revelry with the rest of her brood. Between the alcohol and the fact that there was no sign of Wesley, she had finally begun to relax, allowing herself to enjoy the moment.

The master of ceremonies, a man they called Velvet, stepped into the spotlight. He wore a neatly tailored tuxedo, black dress shoes polished to a high shine and one very sexy smile. When he spoke, his voice was liquid butter, warm and slick and sizzling with an intensity that had every woman in the room fervent with anticipation.

His voice rang loudly around the room. "Good evening, ladies! And welcome to The Wet Bar!"

Another squeal of excitement resonated through the audience.

"For those of you here with us for the first time, sit back, relax and let us show you a good time. If you're back for another helping, well, sit back, relax and let us show you a good time! And we have some serious surprises for all of you tonight. So put your hands together and help me welcome to the stage The Wet Bar's newest performer! They call him Wild Child!"

The music suddenly thumped, Rihanna's "Rude Boy" vibrating around the space. Wild Child made his entrance doing an acrobatic routine, a series of back flips and handsprings that landed him at the foot of the runway. He wore a denim baseball jacket, tear-away denim jeans and work boots. He was bare-chested with the youthful appearance of Baby Face and the body of the Hulk. The women went crazy, screaming their appreciation as he teased and taunted them. Dollar bills were being thrown from every direction and it was obvious that Wild Child was having a great time.

From where they stood on the back side of the mirror both Wesley and Bryan nodded their approval.

"He is good!" Wesley said.

"Two left feet when we give him choreography, but he can freestyle like a beast!"

"Can he go thirty minutes, though?"

"A good twenty, and then we'll have a little intermission before I take the floor."

Wesley nodded, turning to stare back at the performance. "Well, clearly the women love him."

"He's a money maker! Ten more like him and we will truly be golden!"

The crowd was thick and lively. The lights were dimmed, with just a spotlight on their new star attraction. All Wesley could see was an abundance of hair waving, hips thrusting and bodies gyrating. He moved to his phone on the desk and dialed Kamaya's number one more time. And one more time there was no answer, the call going directly to voice mail. It would only be for a few more minutes, he mused. It wasn't what he wanted to do, but he would do what was necessary. He couldn't imagine that Kamaya would be so upset. He blew one more sigh and headed to the dancers' dressing room to change.

Chapter 13

Kamaya laughed, the wealth of it billowing from her midsection. She shook her head, tears misting her eyes. The show wasn't what she had expected and not what Wesley had described. There hadn't been one hint of the group numbers that she knew them to lead with, and the men who typically walked the floor during intermission, working up the crowd, were nowhere to be found. Twice she had tried to excuse herself from the table to sneak into the area designated for employees to try and locate Wesley and twice Tarah had followed on her heels. After that she'd had one drink too many and suddenly nothing at all bothered her.

"Look!" Tarah squealed excitedly, jumping up and down in her seat. "It's the naked man!" she exclaimed, pointing to where Bryan was gyrating for a small crowd of women surrounding him.

The sisters all laughed.

"That's it, you girls have had more than enough," Katherine exclaimed. "That's no man! That's a cowboy!"

Kamaya erupted in laughter for the umpteenth time. She held her stomach as Katrina leaned her head on her shoulder. They were having a good time, and she was glad that things were going well.

Velvet moved back to the microphone. "Let's give the White Prince one last round of applause," he said, his deep baritone caressing the audience like silk.

Bryan jumped back onto the stage and took a deep sweeping bow. His male member stood at full salute, and as Tarah ceremoniously pointed it out to them, laughter rang around the table in abundance.

There was a low drum roll that suddenly filled the air, moving the entire room to fall into a quiet lull.

"We promised you something very special tonight!" Velvet crooned. "Something so incredible that it will have you ladies talking about it for ages to come. When our next performer retired, you all begged him to come back! For years you have been wanting and wishing for him to grace you with his presence, and tonight your dreams have been answered. He's the king of kings, the ultimate dancing sensation and he's come out of retirement for tonight *only*!"

Someone in the back corner suddenly screamed, jumping up and down with so much exuberance that everyone around her bristled with excitement.

Kamaya suddenly shifted forward in her seat, shooting her sister Maitlyn a look.

Maitlyn's eyes widened, meeting her sister's stare.

"What?" she mouthed, a grin suddenly pulling at her full lips.

Kamaya shook her head, her gaze narrow as she flicked her attention back to the stage.

Velvet continued. "Ladies, let's welcome the man of the hour, our very own crown prince, the man you love to love, Deuces!"

The roar in the room was thunderous. Katherine, Katrina and Tarah were on their feet clapping their hands excitedly. Both were caught up in the fervor that rippled from table to table. Kamaya's mouth dropped open, her stunned expression had to have been comical. The color drained from her face and she looked like she'd just lost her very best friend. Beside her, Maitlyn was laughing hysterically, amusement dancing to its own drum.

Wesley stood behind the black velvet curtains with his head bowed. He had always said a quick prayer before stepping out in front of an audience and this time was no different. Few knew that for a brief moment, before every performance, there was a tinge of vulnerability that flickered in his midsection. That moment of prayer was spiritual courage, enabling him to step out and be the public persona his legions of fans believed him to be. For the first few years, dancing past that insecurity had been a struggle, eventually becoming just a job that he did exceptionally well.

This time he prayed that he was doing the right thing for the right reasons and that he didn't embarrass himself having been out of practice for as long as he had. He also prayed that Kamaya would be understanding and that they could eventually make jokes about his reemergence. He prayed, and then Velvet announced his stage name and the noise level in the room rose tenfold.

The room went dark. A low hush billowed through the air, rising like a sweet morning mist. Kamaya could feel the women around the room beginning to stand in anticipation.

One spotlight suddenly flashed on the center of the stage. Wesley stood there, dressed in a classically tailored black tuxedo, the white dress shirt unbuttoned down his chest, a gentleman's fedora perched on his head. His face was tilted downward and the fingers of his right hand traced the brim of his hat. He was snapping the fingers of his left hand, one foot tapping in time to set the beat, and then the music started.

Kamaya felt her breath catch deep in her chest and hold. Wesley was absolutely breathtaking. He stood tall and imposing, his height and size seeming even more impressive. He was the most luscious drink of dark chocolate, and every woman in the room suddenly wanted a sip. Her eyes skated back and forth, eyeing the crowd who were ogling him like he was the best thing since sliced bread. Every one of them had dropped into the fantasy of the man, lost completely in raw, unadulterated desire.

Maitlyn leaned near and whispered her name. "Breathe, Kamaya," she said. "You need to breathe!"

"He said he wasn't dancing," Kamaya hissed between clenched teeth. "Why is he *dancing*?"

Maitlyn giggled. "Because he's damn good at it!"

"Oh, he is better than good!" Tarah interjected, she and Katrina giggling like school kids.

Kamaya tossed her sisters a quick look, took a deep

inhale of air and then she turned her attention back to the stage. Wesley's song of choice was "No Diggity" by Blackstreet, the deep rhythmic thump of the beat seeming to take full and complete control of Wesley's body.

As Dr. Dre dropped the first verse, Wesley tossed his hat across the room, slinging it like a Frisbee to one of the waiters who caught it easily and nestled it atop a customer's head. The woman looked like she'd just won the golden ticket as she jumped up and down excitedly. He worked the width of the stage in time to the music, his movements like the most sensual caress.

As the song played, Wesley gyrated left and then right, his body moving so succinctly that it was if he himself *was* the music. It was a slow, seductive striptease, as he came out of his jacket first and then his shirt. Bare-chested he strutted back and forth, his swagger so on point that he had every woman around Kamaya salivating. When he reached the first chorus he'd sashayed right out of his slacks, wearing the barest pair of Speedos that accentuated every vein and muscle of his male member which was engorged to sheer magnificence.

Kamaya gasped. His arms were raised over his head, his hips shifting from side to side. He rocked forward thrusting himself in one direction and then another, backing his buttocks up so sensually that the room went wild.

"DEUCE!" someone screamed from the back of the room. "I love you, Deuce!"

The music track shifted swiftly from one song to another, moving to Montel Jordan and "This Is How We Do It" and then the SOS Band's "Take Your Time." Wesley brought a playful flair to his movements and then the lights lifted enough for him to move from the stage to the floor. He was putting on quite the show as he got up close but just a touch too personal, Kamaya thought, with his customers.

Salt-N-Pepa's "Push It" had just come on when Wesley spun from one table to theirs and saw Kamaya for the first time. His eyes widened, but he didn't miss a beat, his pelvic thrusts moving of their own volition. His gaze skated from her to her siblings and then her mother, and that's when his cheeks heated with embarrassment. He couldn't spin in the opposite direction fast enough, and as he turned, Katherine reached out and smacked him sharply on his ass.

Kamaya closed her eyes, her head moving from side to side. When she opened them, Wesley had moved himself to the other side of the room, still dancing, still the consummate performer.

She stood up abruptly, her eyes glazed. "We should go," she said as she gestured for their waiter and the bill.

His sisters were all eyeing her intently, not missing that the moment was a sensitive one for her.

Her mother broke the tension. "Kamaya, I think when we get home we might need to have a conversation about that new boyfriend of yours!"

It was barely five minutes later when Bryan signaled for Wesley's attention, motioning for him to take his last bow. Goldberg was dressed and ready, waiting to perform his fire and hose routine. With one last hip thrust, Wesley took a bow, blowing kisses as the curtain dropped in front of him. The room was screaming for an encore but there was no way he was going back for a second round.

Bryan tapped him on the back. "Those women missed themselves some Deuce! They love you!"

Wesley shook his head, stomping back to his office where he slammed the door. He reached for the phone and dialed Kamaya's number. When it went to voice mail again he slammed the receiver back onto the hook, a string of profanity flying past his lips.

Bryan rushed into the room behind him. "What's wrong?"

"Did you see Kamaya? Did you know she was here?"

Bryan shook his head, moving to the mirrored window. "Kamaya is here?" he questioned, his eyes searching through the crowd.

"Well, she's not now! She left after her mother slapped me on my ass."

Bryan fought to contain his amusement. "Her mother slapped you on the ass?"

Wesley shook his head. "I think it was her mother. I don't know. I just…" He slammed a fist on the desk. "Oh, my God! What just happened?"

"You just killed it, is what just happened."

"I just danced in front of my girl's entire family! Her sisters *and* her mother. Her mother! That's like shaking my package and dancing in front of *my* mother. That's not cool, dude! It's her effing family!"

"Her daddy wasn't here too, was he?"

The look Wesley gave his friend was cold, edged in barbed wire and ice. "I'm not in the mood for jokes right now. I am so not in the mood." He reached for the phone and dialed Kamaya's number one more time.

Kamaya wasn't answering her phone. Wesley had tried her multiple times but she had gone radio silent.

Her silence had begun to irritate him. He understood that she was upset, but there was no way either could fix what was broken if she refused to talk to him. Frustration furrowed his brow as he slammed his cell phone back to his desktop.

It had been a good few days since his performance. And suddenly he was an internet sensation, the performance captured on video and viewed more times than he cared to count. He had no doubts the titillation was why the crowds had doubled, the club filled to capacity six nights out of six. Everyone wanted Deuce to come back again and that wasn't going to happen.

His return hadn't been his brightest idea. The necessity of it notwithstanding, he should have talked to Kamaya first. He should have gotten her input on the craziness of the idea. But his judgment had been compromised and he had acted out of fear; nervous that the night would have been a failure. Or had he?

The more he thought about it, the less he was inclined to beat himself up over doing what he needed to do. He couldn't afford for the business to take a hit, and a club with no talent could have easily been the kiss of death. Patrons would much rather spend their money where they might be pleasantly surprised than spend their money and be wholeheartedly disappointed. Disappointment equaled low sales and he was all about his money. He had to be. His ambition couldn't be curtailed. He knew if anyone could understand that, Kamaya could. If only she would pick up the phone and talk to him!

After lectures from her parents, her sisters, her brothers and her nail technician, Kamaya had taken to her bed, pulling the covers over her head and refusing to engage with anyone. She'd taken the battery out of her phone and didn't bother to go to the door the few times Wesley had come knocking. She thought back to her mother and the conversation that had followed after that disastrous night.

"Kamaya, did you know he was a dancer?" Katherine had asked on the car ride home. "I thought he owned a club?"

"*Was* is the operative word. He *was* a dancer. He told me he put that behind him and I believed him," she'd snapped.

Katherine had nodded her head, cutting an eye at Maitlyn who was steering them toward home. "Clearly, you all knew he used to dance. Is that right?"

Tarah had giggled. "Looked like he's still dancing, and dancing quite well, if I might add."

Kamaya had glared at her sister then turned to stare out the car window.

"It would seem that you two might have some communication issues," her mother had said matter-of-factly. "You might want to talk to him."

"That's not going to happen," Kamaya had snapped. "I don't have anything to say to him. Nothing!"

That had made Katherine laugh. "Okay, nothing. Let me know how that conversation goes when you do have it."

Kamaya shook herself out of the trance she'd dropped into. She couldn't begin to explain why Wesley being on that stage disturbed her. When she'd gotten home and found all his phone messages, she'd realized he had tried earnestly to reach her, anxious to tell her something. She realized he had not intended for her to be caught off guard by that something. But she had been, and for reasons she didn't understand, it all felt like a deep punch to her gut. A punch she was having a hard time recovering from.

She suddenly sat upright. She reached for the cell phone that rested on the nightstand, replaced the battery and dialed. Just seconds later Maitlyn answered.

"What's wrong?" her sister asked. In the background, the new baby cried, the sound low and pitiful.

"Why is Zakar crying? Is he okay?"

"He is just fine. He wants back on the breast and he's going to have to get over it."

"Is he hungry?"

"No, he nurses until he's full, then he wants to stay latched on like I don't have anything else to do. He'll be sound asleep in a few minutes."

"If you say so."

"He's going to be a breast man like his daddy."

"Way more information than I needed to know."

"So what's wrong with you?"

Kamaya paused, hesitating briefly as she chose her words carefully. "Why am I so ready to push Wesley away and throw what we have in the trash?"

Maitlyn blew a soft sigh. "Because you love him and you're scared."

"I don't... I..."

Her sister laughed. "You love him and there's nothing wrong with that, Kamaya. He loves you and what you two have is a beautiful thing when you allow it to be."

"Maybe that's true, and I'm not saying it is, but... well...why does that frighten me so much? Because it truly scares the hell out of me!"

"Because it means you have to give up control, or at least share it with someone else."

Kamaya took a deep breath and held it for a good long minute before finally blowing it past her lips. "Thanks," she said finally. "I need to think about what you said."

"I have a question for you," Maitlyn said. The background was now quiet, the baby asleep as her sister had predicted.

"What's that?"

"Why haven't you told us about your adult businesses?"

"Excuse me?"

"You heard me! You have some serious investments in the sex industry and you've been keeping everyone in the dark like we wouldn't find out."

"Why would you think something like that?" Kamaya asked, her tone hardly convincing.

"Really? Now you're going to play dumb?"

"Why are you all up in my business?"

"You're the one who asked me to investigate your boyfriend. You didn't think that I wouldn't put two and two together? Once I discovered his connection to the franchise I dug a little deeper. When your boy Paxton's name came up under all that dirt, it all just made sense. Paxton isn't smart enough to build that kind of profile all on his own. No offense."

"None taken."

"So why the lies and the secrecy?"

"Because your parents would have a fit! And I could just imagine what Mason would have to say."

"They wouldn't be happy, but they'd support your

decisions, especially if you chose to explain your rationale for doing what you're doing."

"*Oh, Senior, I sell sex toys because they make me money!* I can just imagine his reaction to that conversation!"

"You really don't give them any credit, but if it's any consolation, Mason already knows, so I wouldn't be surprised if the old people know, too. They're probably just waiting for the right time to say something."

"You told Mason?"

"Mason told me. He was concerned that maybe business wasn't going well for you and he was thinking about giving you an infusion of cash to help you out. He found out about the sex toys and the vaginal rejuvenation centers. He probably doesn't know about the strip bars yet. But I'm sure that's only a matter of time after he hears about your boyfriend's dance moves!"

"I really don't like you right now. And I really don't like this family. All of you are too damn nosey!"

"We love you, too!"

"So what do I do know?"

"Get your guy back. Let the rest work itself out."

"You make it sound so easy."

"It is easy, Kamaya. If you love Wesley. Just tell him so!"

Annie Walters stared at her son, her expression blank as he explained to his parents why they had yet to meet Kamaya since arriving in New Orleans. He made no false excuses, telling his mother and father the truth.

Leon Walters shook his head. "Well, now. I'm not sure what to say about all that, son."

Annie pursed her lips as she folded her hands in her

lap. She still hadn't said anything at all, but there was no missing that a lot was suddenly flashing through her mind as she looked from one to the other.

Wesley took a deep inhale of air. "I'm sorry. I knew if I told you how I was earning my money when I was in school that you wouldn't have approved and you would have made me stop."

Annie nodded. "Yes, I probably would have told you that I disapproved, but you are an adult so I also would have told you that you needed to do what was best for you. But I definitely can't say that taking your clothes off for women in a bar is best for anyone."

"And you're still doing this exotic dancing thing?" Leon questioned.

Wesley vehemently shook his head. "No, sir. I do own a club, but I employ other men who are dancers. The only reason I danced the night Kamaya saw me was because of an emergency."

His father nodded. "Well, you had to do what you had to do, I guess."

Annie shook her head. "Lord have mercy, that poor girl. That was a lot for her to have to take in! Her man shaking his goodies like that. And I can just imagine what her mother had to say. With her in the church, too! You did apologize, I hope?"

He shook his head. "Kamaya won't talk to me and I haven't tried to reach out to anyone in her family."

"That's your first mistake, Wesley, and I know I raised you better than that. You also owe her mother an apology. And you need to speak to her father about your behavior. How can he give his approval when you're out here acting like you've had no home training?"

Wesley shook his head. "Ma, it's not like…"

Leon shook his head, interrupting as he pointed his index finger at his son. "Obviously, this young woman's family is important to her, and if that's so, then you need to plead your case with them, too. Besides, if you love this girl like you say you do, then you need to go sit down with her father and let him know your intentions. It's only right."

"Do what your father says, Wesley, then invite Mr. and Mrs. Boudreaux to dinner. "I'm going to fry them some chicken and make some potato salad. Leon, we need to go to the supermarket." The matriarch moved in the direction of the door, grabbing her purse as she made her exit.

"Whatever you need, Annie!" his father replied, sauntering slowly after her. He paused, tossing a quick glance toward the door before turning back to his son. He chuckled warmly, giving Wesley a thumbs-up and a wink. "You're a chip off the old block!"

His wife suddenly called his name. "Leon!"

"What?" He snapped back around to see Annie glaring at him.

"You gyrating to James Brown in the middle of the bathroom with your socks on is way different from what Wesley did. Come get in this car!"

Leon winked a second time then turned to leave.

"Wesley?" his mother called.

"Yes, ma'am?"

"Call Kamaya. Fix this."

He blew a heavy sigh and nodded his head. "Yes, ma'am."

Chapter 14

As Kamaya pulled up in front of Wesley's home, she couldn't miss the luxury Mercedes parked in the driveway. Or the tall blonde woman who stood at the edge of the property peering through the fence into the rear yard. Neither Wesley nor his blue hooptie were anywhere to be seen.

Kamaya stepped out of her own car and gave the woman a look. The two eyed each other, reserve washing over their expressions. Kamaya spoke first.

"Can I help you?"

The blonde woman eyed her from head to toe. "I'm looking for Wesley."

"I'm his girlfriend. Can I help you?"

"I'm Carrie. I have something to give him."

Kamaya paused for a quick second. "He's not home, but you can leave whatever it is with me. I'll make sure he gets it."

The woman smiled, her haughty expression prickling Kamaya's spirit.

"Thanks, but I can't give it to you," she said, and then she sauntered past Kamaya to her car. She slid her lean frame into the driver's seat of that Mercedes, engaged the engine and backed out into the street.

Kamaya felt her mood swing toward annoyance as she watched the woman shift the car into drive and disappear around the corner. She dropped one hand to her hip. *Who the hell was that?* she wondered. Jealousy wafted from deep in the pit of her stomach. *Was Wesley actually entertaining other women already? Had he moved on from their relationship that easily?* After thinking the absolute worst and taking a moment to ponder why she was even there, she moved back to her own car and headed back across town.

Wesley pulled past the wrought-iron gates of the Boudreaux's Broadway Street home and parked his car. He sat for a few minutes trying to gather his thoughts, hoping that what he was about to do wouldn't turn out to be a disaster. He had called first, so he knew that Katherine and Senior were expecting him. As he stepped out of his car and engaged the alarm, the front door swung open and Kamaya's father waved him inside.

"It's good to see you, son!" the older man intoned. "I hope you're doing well?"

"I am. Thank you for asking, sir. I appreciate you and your wife taking the time to speak with me."

"Not a problem at all. It sounded important."

Wesley nodded. "I'm sure you know I'm not your daughter's favorite person right now."

Senior laughed. "Kamaya doesn't have many favorite people, son! I warned you she's a hard bird when she wants to be!"

His gut-deep laugh calmed Wesley's nerves slightly. He smiled and laughed with the man.

"Come on inside and take a seat. I'll go find my wife!"

"Thank you, sir!"

While he waited, Wesley sat in the living room of the Boudreaux family home, twisting his hands nervously together in his lap. Minutes later, Kamaya's parents sat on the sofa opposite him, both eyeing him with keen stares. He had been rambling for longer than necessary and knew that he needed to get to the point and explain why he was there. He took a deep breath.

"Mrs. Boudreaux, I want to apologize for what happened the other night. I…well…"

"What happened the other night?" Senior asked, cutting an eye at his wife.

Katherine held up her hand, halting her husband's comments. "You were working. That, I understand completely. Kamaya should have prepared me and her sisters, but she and I have already had a conversation about that."

"Prepared y'all for what?" Senior queried.

Wesley and Katherine traded gazes. She gave him a warming smile. "That's not for me to say, Senior," she answered.

Senior shifted his gaze toward Wesley. "Well, someone is going to tell me something," he commanded.

Wesley took a deep breath and swallowed hard. He continued to wring his hands together in his lap. He shook his head slightly before he spoke. "Mr. Boudreaux, the club I own is a male strip club called The Wet Bar."

"It's not a jazz bar?"

"No, sir. It's an adult entertainment business that caters to a professional female clientele."

"So, y'all are like them boys in New York. Them Chipmunks?"

Katherine laughed. "Chippendales!" she said.

"Y'all are like them Chippendales?" Senior asked.

"Yes, sir."

Senior shot a look at his wife. "Is that where them girls took you for your birthday? To a strip club?"

Katherine chuckled. "Yes, they did."

Senior rolled his eyes. He shifted his gaze back to stare at Wesley, his eyebrows raised. "So what happened that you need to apologize to my wife?"

Wesley took another breath. "That night, most of my dancers didn't show up for work and…well…I had to step in and perform. I wasn't anticipating Kamaya, or her mother, being there."

There was a moment of pause and then Senior suddenly burst out laughing. "I bet that was a sight!"

Katherine smiled. "It was something all right."

Heat tinted Wesley's cheeks a deep, deep shade of embarrassment. He didn't bother to respond.

"So that's why Kamaya's not talking to you, huh?"

"Yes, sir. She's not happy with me. I'm praying that she'll give me an opportunity to explain."

Senior nodded, his head moving slowly up and down. His hands were folded together in his lap. He gestured toward his wife with his eyes. "Katherine, can you give us a minute, please? I'd like to talk to Wesley, man-to-man."

"I'll go fix us all some tea and cinnamon crumb cake," she said, as she rose from her seat. When she passed by Wesley, she ran a warm palm over his shoulder, the gesture meant to be comforting.

Wesley felt himself sink into the warmth, appreciating the gesture of kindness. As the matriarch disappeared into the kitchen, he locked gazes with Kamaya's father. His stomach suddenly did a flip and he inhaled swiftly to stall the sudden rise of anxiety that had kicked that comfort to the curb.

Senior stood up, moving to the mantel over the fireplace. He pulled one of their family portraits from its resting spot, taking a quick moment to study the faces of his children. A slow smile pulled at his mouth, and pride and joy shimmered in his dark eyes.

He turned and passed the framed image to Wesley, dropping into the seat beside the young man. He sat silently as he watched as Wesley studied the picture just as he had. The photo had been taken in Italy, when the family had converged on Maremma in Tuscany for Donovan's marriage to Gianna Martelli. Smiles were abundant as he and his wife sat with all of their children flanking them, a grove of olive trees in the background.

"Son, if you're lucky, one day you and whoever you marry are going to sit together and look back on those things that brought you together and kept you together. You're going to laugh about moments that, at the time, you thought would break you, and you're going to shed a tear or two over memories that kept you holding it all together. You're going to thank God for your blessings and you're going to start with your children. I do it every day. Every day." His smile lifted again as he reached for the picture, pulling it from Wesley's hands.

"I know that you care about my daughter. And I respect that you were man enough to come here to talk to me and my wife. I wasn't there to see what happened and that's probably a good thing. But had my Katherine been offended, she would have told you. She has never been one to bite her tongue, especially if it concerns our children.

"Now, I'm not going to lie to you. You working as a stripper, now or even before, doesn't sit well with me. And I can't say that I'm comfortable with my daughter dating a former dancer, or a current one, but my baby girl being happy is more important to me than what you do for a living. If she likes it, I'll learn to love it! But don't think I won't address any concerns I have with you, or her."

Wesley nodded. "I can appreciate that, sir."

"Make no mistake about it, Wesley. Katherine and I weren't born yesterday. Our children may think we're out of touch, but there is very little that they do, or don't do, that we don't know about. We also know that every one of them tries to keep some things secret, and while they might, we know our kids and we know what they need even before they do.

"Kamaya needs a man who's willing to be her partner, who doesn't mind allowing her to think that she's in charge even when she isn't. A man who's good to her, first and foremost, and who's confident enough in himself to not be intimidated by her and her success.

"I think you have the potential to be that man but it's not something you can rush, son. If you hope to be sitting here one day, talking to some boy about how he loves one of my grandbabies, showing off pictures of you and Kamaya's family, you just need to take your time in letting things work out. When it should, it will!"

Wesley pondered Senior's comments for a brief moment and then he nodded his head. "I love her, sir. I love your daughter very much."

"I know."

"I'm praying that, when we get past all of this, Kamaya will marry me and that you and Mrs. Boudreaux will give us your approval."

"You do know that Kamaya is the one child of ours who doesn't seek out our approval for her choices, don't you?"

Wesley smiled. "I know that your approval is more important to her than even she realizes. And it's definitely very important to me, sir!"

Senior extended his hand. The two men shook. "Smells like my Katherine done took that cake out of the oven!" The scent of cinnamon, vanilla and sugar danced through the air.

Kamaya stomped into her mother's kitchen, her attitude following her. She slammed her body down onto one of the cushioned chairs, thoughts of the woman she'd seen at Wesley's house still irritating her nerves.

"Excuse me?" Katherine snapped, a hand falling against the line of her full hips.

"Sorry," Kamaya apologized. "I wasn't trying to be rude. Good afternoon!"

"Good afternoon. I was starting to think that you forgot all of your home training!"

"No, I just...well..." Kamaya blew a soft sigh. "I'm frustrated and I don't know what to do," she finally said, telling her mother about her visit to Wesley's home.

Katherine laughed. "Kamaya, you are redefining the term drama queen! What is wrong with you, baby?"

Tears suddenly misted Kamaya's eyes. "I don't know, Mama. I really don't know. I just can't seem to get it together lately."

"Is this about Wesley?"

Kamaya shrugged. She dropped her head, her chin grazing her chest. "I miss him," she finally whispered. "But I'm still mad at him."

"What are you actually mad about?"

"I don't know. I know he wasn't trying to hide the fact that he danced from me. In fact, I know he tried hard to tell me before he did it but…we…" She shrugged her shoulders and blew another sigh.

"You were jealous. You were jealous that your man made quite the impression on a room full of women who got to see him in a way you didn't like."

Kamaya shrugged again. "It was that and it's… well…" She hesitated a second time, lifting her gaze to meet her mother's. "I love him. But I don't want to love him and be afraid that what we do for a living is going to be a problem for us in the long run."

"Have you been honest with him, Kamaya? Have you told him how you feel?"

Kamaya shrugged her narrow shoulders one more time. "He knows. I may not have said all the words everyone else thinks I should say, but he gets me."

Her mother shook her head. "Your daddy and I have worried about all of you kids. We used to be afraid that Tarah was never going to grow up and learn to depend on herself. We worried that Maitlyn would never let her walls down to allow herself be loved. We worried that Mason was always going to put work before everything else. We worried about each of you because that's what parents do. But you…well…we still worry that you trying to do what you think we want is going to keep you from having the happiness you deserve."

"I don't do that. I don't…"

Her mother shook her head. "Kamaya, since you were a little girl you've been trying to walk in everyone else's footsteps instead of forging your own. You keep your life from us because you're afraid that you'll be judged or that we will disapprove. I have been telling you since you were two, just be yourself! Be honest and truthful and just be you! We will always love you no matter what. But a man can't love you if you don't let him see who you really are—not what you think he wants to see. If Wesley's dancing is bothersome to you, then you need to say so. Don't make it about me or your sisters and how we feel about it."

"But it doesn't bother me. Not really."

"Then you need to ask yourself what's going on that has you so out of sorts. You need to be honest with yourself if you're not honest with anyone else."

Katherine moved back to the counter to check the cake she'd just pulled from the oven. Its decadent aroma swept through the home, teasing Kamaya's senses. Her mother reached into the cabinets, pulled down a stack of plates and proceeded to set the table for four people.

Kamaya suddenly eyed her mother curiously. "I'm sorry. Are you expecting company?"

Katherine chuckled softly. "Company is already here. Wesley's in the living room talking with your father. And you're here. I thought it would be nice for the four of us to sit and have some tea and cake."

Kamaya's eyes widened. "Wesley is here? Why didn't you tell me?"

"I thought you would have noticed his car parked in my driveway."

Kamaya jumped to her feet and moved to the window. Sure enough Wesley's hooptie was parked across the street in front of the home. She'd been so frantic when she arrived that she hadn't even noticed. Her eyes skated back and forth, her mind suddenly racing. "I should probably..."

"You should pull some silverware out of the drawer. I'll let the boys know the tea is ready."

"But I don't want..."

Katherine gave her daughter a stern look. She didn't need to voice the comment seeping from her eyes. Kamaya closed her mouth and reached into the cabinet drawer for four forks and four spoons. She grabbed napkins from a drawer and completed the place settings her mother had started.

Just minutes later Wesley and Senior moved through the kitchen door. "It sure smells good in here!" Senior exclaimed as he moved to his wife's side and kissed her cheek. He winked at his daughter. "Hey, baby!"

"Hey, Senior." She tossed a quick look in Wesley's direction. "Hey," she said softly.

He smiled as he sauntered to her side. He eased his fingers into her hair and pressed his lips to her forehead. "Hey," he whispered back, his gaze connecting with hers.

"What are you doing here?" she asked, cutting a quick eye toward her parents, who were both watching them intently.

"I needed to speak with your parents."

Katherine interrupted the conversation. "Come sit down you two. This cake is still nice and warm. Do either of you want ice cream to go with it?"

Kamaya shook her head. "No, thank you."

Wesley grinned. "I would," he answered. "If it's not too much trouble."

"No trouble at all!" Katherine replied.

"I'll take some vanilla ice cream, too!" Senior interjected as he pulled a seat up to the kitchen table.

"Can you please excuse us for a minute?" Kamaya asked, looking from her father to her mother. She grabbed Wesley by the hand. "It'll only take a minute," she said as she pulled him along behind her, heading toward the living room.

"I expect that boy to come back here in one piece!" Senior shouted after them. "I mean it, Kamaya!"

Kamaya could hear her mother's distinct laugher.

"I'm sorry," Kamaya said, as she pressed her mouth to Wesley's, kissing him eagerly.

Wesley kissed her back, folding his arms around her. "So am I," he said, when they finally came up for air. "I tried to call you, Kamaya. That night. I tried to call to let you know what was going on. I didn't mean for you to find out like that. I would never intentionally disrespect you or your family. You should know that."

"I do know. And, I overreacted. But seeing you like that…dancing…well…it…" She hesitated. "It pissed me off!" she said finally. "You swore to me that you would only dance for me and no one else. You promised."

A slow bend lifted his full lips into a wide smile. "You were jealous?"

"I said I was pissed!" She took a step back from him,

folding her arms over her chest. "Don't make me promises if you don't intend to keep them. I want to trust you and I can't if you don't keep your word."

Wesley pondered her comment. He turned to stare out the window for a brief moment before spinning himself back toward her. He swept her back into his arms and kissed her again. "I love you, Kamaya, and I swear on everything I hold sacred that I will never again break any promise I make to you. And I won't make you any promises that I know I can't keep."

Kamaya nodded as he continued.

"But I need something from you," Wesley said. His gaze was direct, searing, as he stared into her eyes. "I actually need two things."

"Anything!"

"First, if you ever ignore me again, that's going to be a problem for both of us. I can't be in a relationship with a woman who won't talk to me."

"I was angry and I didn't want to say something I regretted."

"I don't care. If you love me, then you say whatever it is you think you need to say. And then we'll talk. But we will never be able to fix anything if you shut me out."

Kamaya took a deep breath. She nodded her head slowly. "I really am sorry. I really regret how I've been acting. You deserve better than that from me."

"One more thing."

She held up her hand to stall his comment. "Before you finish, who's Carrie?"

"Carrie?" A hint of surprise shimmered across Wesley's face. "Where did you…"

"She was at your house looking for you this morning."

"You were at my house this morning?"

"I wanted to apologize. I went there to talk to you so that we could figure things out. Your friend Carrie was there when I arrived."

Wesley nodded. "Carrie is an old friend. I'm sure she was just there to drop something off."

"That's what she said. But she wouldn't tell me what it was and she said she couldn't leave it with me."

"Carrie's like that. Don't take it personal."

Kamaya shrugged. "So, what's the second thing you need from me?"

"No more secrets. You and I both need to come clean to the people who love us most. I told my parents about what happened and about the club, the business and my dancing. I need for you to tell your parents the truth about everything, too. Because I love you I can't keep lying for you. We can't keep lying. It's not who I am. And it's not who you are, either."

A veil of tension suddenly billowed between them, and then her mother's words echoed loudly through her head. *I have been telling you since you were two, just be yourself! Be honest and truthful and just be you! We will always love you no matter what.*

Kamaya had kept her life from her family. Unlike her twin brother, who had done the same in order to protect the family from his responsibilities as a CIA agent, she had done so because she hadn't wanted any of her family to be disappointed. She had wanted her parents to be as proud of her as she knew they were proud of Mason and Maitlyn and the rest of her siblings with their many, many accomplishments. She'd been fearful of upsetting the family balance and tarnishing the legacy of the Boudreaux name. Fear had been holding her back from many things.

Her gaze reconnected with Wesley's. "We should get back. Your ice cream is melting."

Kamaya heard her sister calling out to her as Maitlyn let herself into the family home. Her father was still bellowing at her, his index finger waving back and forth with his narrative. As Maitlyn came into the room Kamaya shot her sister a look, wanting to forewarn her that Ma and Pa Boudreaux were not happy campers.

"Hey, there!" Maitlyn sang out. She waved a slight hand as she locked eyes with each of them. "What's going on?"

Senior twisted in his seat to face her. "Did you know your sister owns a bunch of sex shops?"

Kamaya rolled her eyes. "They are not sex shops!" she exclaimed for the umpteenth time.

Katherine shot a look in her direction, her head moving from side to side.

Maitlyn took a deep breath. "I am very aware of Kamaya's business investments. She's consulted with me on most of them."

Kamaya's gaze skated in Maitlyn's direction. Her sister gave her a smile.

"And you didn't tell us?" their father queried.

"Kamaya didn't want everyone involved in her business decisions and I had to respect that. Besides, it wasn't my place to tell you."

Senior turned his attention back to his other daughter, continuing where he'd left off in their conversation. "Kamaya, your mother and I have not always agreed with the things you and your brothers and sisters have done, but we never expected that you would think that you couldn't trust us to support you."

"It wasn't about trusting you, Senior. I just didn't think you'd understand, and I didn't want to embarrass you or Mom."

"You do know that we love you, right?" Katherine said softly.

Kamaya nodded. "Of course."

Wesley interjected. "Senior, Kamaya and I needed to be honest with you both. And my parents, too. We know we can't build a successful relationship without telling everyone the truth. Our families can't support us if they don't know what we're up against." He squeezed Kamaya's hand, drawing the back of her fingers to his lips and kissing them.

Senior nodded. "And what does Mason think? I know you asked Mason for help, right?"

Kamaya shook her head. "No, sir. I didn't. I built this business all on my own."

Maitlyn moved to Kamaya's side, dropping her hand against her sister's shoulder. "Kamaya's net worth should make you *very* proud. She took everything you and Mom taught her and she didn't need to lean on her brothers or any other man to help her accomplish her goals. Had she opened up to you, or Mason, or anyone, you all would have tried to influence her decisions. This way, her mistakes were hers and no one else's."

Katherine nodded. "And her accomplishments are hers, as well. No one else's!" she said, beaming excitedly. "That's my girl!"

The room grew silent, everyone falling into their own thoughts. Minutes passed before Senior suddenly moved onto his feet at Kamaya's side. He hugged her close as he kissed her cheek.

"You're going to have to explain that vaginal rejuvenation to me. That don't make no kind of sense!"

Kamaya winced, a blush of color warming her cheeks. "I'll bring you a brochure."

Senior winked at Katherine. "Your mom and I can read it together. Might come in handy!"

The matriarch laughed heartily. "Senior, I know you have lost your mind!"

Chapter 15

It had been a long day. Too long. But in spite of everything, Kamaya felt happier than she had in a very long time. Opening up to her mother and father had gone better than she could have ever anticipated. Their support had been unwavering, and suddenly having no secrets to keep had Kamaya feeling like a new woman.

She rinsed the dish she'd just washed, sliding it into the drying rack. Wesley's mother patted her gently against her back. "You okay, baby?" she asked.

Kamaya nodded. "Yes, ma'am. I'm really good."

Annie smiled. "It was so nice to meet your mama and daddy. I'm so glad you all could come have dinner with us."

"We appreciate you inviting us. And the food was so good. You'll have to teach me how to fry chicken like that so I can cook it for Wesley."

"I'd love to show you. Fried chicken is his favorite, you know."

Kamaya laughed. "I think anything you cook is his favorite!"

Annie laughed with her. "You make him very happy, Kamaya. And that makes me very happy."

"Thank you. He's an incredible man. I'm very, very lucky."

"That you are!"

The two women continued chatting until the last dirty dish had been washed, dried and put away. Wesley had wanted them to use his dishwasher, but his mother had insisted on hand washing them, giving the two women an opportunity to spend some quality time together.

"What are you two talking about in here?" Wesley asked, moving into the room. He kissed his mother's cheek and then Kamaya's.

"We were comparing notes on our favorite guy!" Kamaya said. She winked at his mother.

Annie laughed. "I didn't know Kamaya knew your daddy that well!" she said teasingly.

"Ha, ha, ha!" Wesley said. "My favorite women both have jokes."

The trio laughed, continuing to banter back and forth. Wesley's father soon joined them.

"I was just about to send out the troops to look for you all. What's going on in here?" Leon asked.

His wife slid herself against his side, wrapping her arms around his waist. "Just spending some time with our future daughter-in-law," she said, as she gave him a squeeze. She winked at her son.

Kamaya and Wesley exchanged a quick look. The

moment was awkward and they both tittered, a nervous chuckle that soon had all four of them laughing heartily.

"I really need to head home," Kamaya said.

"Don't rush off," Wesley said, as he rested a large hand against her waist. His eyes danced with hers, his look practically pleading.

"I have a big day tomorrow," she said as she reached up on her toes to kiss his lips. She moved to where his parents were standing. She hugged Annie first and then Leon. "It really was a pleasure to finally meet you both. I'm sure we'll see each other again soon."

"We look forward to it, young lady," Leon said. "And make sure you tell that father of yours that I can't wait for him and your mama to come to Alabama so I can take him fishing!"

"I'll be sure to tell him," Kamaya responded. She gave them both a slight wave of her hand and turned toward the door.

"Let me walk you to your car," Wesley said. He reached for her hand and entwined his fingers with hers. The two exited the room, his parents grinning brightly behind them.

"I really like your mom and dad," Kamaya said, as they strolled down his driveway toward where her car was parked.

"They like you, too, and that's a good thing. I couldn't be with any woman my mother didn't like."

She smiled. "You are such a mama's boy!"

"That's why you love me."

There was a brief pause, and something Wesley didn't recognize crossed her face. She suddenly locked eyes with him, tears misting her gaze. "I really do love you," she said, her voice a loud whisper. "You know that, right? I love you more than anything else in this world."

Wesley wrapped his arms around Kamaya and pulled her body close to his. He hugged her tightly and then he leaned to press his lips to hers.

The kiss was sweet and tender, the moment solidifying everything that was good between them. They kissed for what felt like an eternity, neither wanting to let the other go. When Kamaya finally pulled away, stepping out of his arms, it felt as if they were both losing a small piece of themselves.

"I'll call you when I get home," she whispered softly.

Wesley nodded. "Baby, you really don't have to leave. My parents will understand."

"Your mother likes me and I'd like to keep it that way," she said, as she gave him one last peck on the mouth. "I'll call."

He chuckled warmly. "They head home tomorrow. Tomorrow night I'm not letting you leave."

Kamaya grinned. "Tomorrow night you won't have to."

The next morning Kamaya dragged herself to the office, the few hours of sleep she'd had fueling her steps. She and Wesley had talked on the phone until the early dawn, planning their future. Dreams fueled what they hoped for themselves and wished for each other. She imagined he was as exhausted as she was.

Virginia met her at the door with a large cup of coffee and a stack of manila folders. "Morning, boss lady!"

"Good morning! Did you get my text message?"

The woman nodded. "Yes, ma'am! I called your sister and everything is being handled."

Kamaya gave her two thumbs-up before reaching for

the coffee mug and the paperwork. "Have you seen…" she started.

"Paxton is in your office waiting for you," Virginia said, her voice dropping to a loud whisper.

Kamaya's gaze narrowed ever so slightly. "What's wrong? What am I missing?"

Virginia shook her head. "He's not alone," she said. "His fiancée is with him."

Kamaya's eyebrows raised slightly. "Well," she said. "Isn't that special?"

Virginia gave her a slight smile and then they both laughed.

Taking a deep breath Kamaya paused at the door to her office. She counted to ten and then let herself inside.

Paxton jumped from his seat, anxiety washing over his expression as he came to his feet. Laney McDonald sat behind Kamaya's desk, casually flipping through the papers that rested on top of the wood surface. Kamaya shot a look toward them both before she spoke.

"Good morning," she said. "To what do I owe the honor?" She moved to where Laney was still sitting like a log in her chair.

"Good morning," Paxton muttered. "Laney, that's Kamaya's chair," he said casually.

The woman giggled. "Kamaya, hello! I apologize! I hope I'm not in the way."

Kamaya forced her mouth into a polite smile. "There's a chair beside Paxton," she said. "Get out of my seat. Please."

Laney giggled again, rising slowly. She eased her way to the other side of the desk and sat down on the arm of Paxton's chair. Kamaya shifted her eyes toward him, her expression giving him fair warning.

Paxton tapped his palm against the chair beside him. "Sweetheart, sit. Make yourself comfortable," he said.

Laney rolled her eyes skyward as she slid into the other chair and crossed her legs.

Kamaya took a seat in her chair, clasping her hands together in front of her. "So, what's up?"

Paxton swallowed. Hard. He looked like he was about to choke on the words he was carefully choosing. Laney reached a manicured hand out and trailed her lengthy fingernails down his thigh. She gave him a bright smile, porcelain veneers gleaming brightly.

It was enough to make Kamaya vomit. "I really have a tight schedule today, Paxton, so spit it out," she said.

He nodded. "I mentioned it briefly the other day. Laney and I are going into business together. We don't think it'll be in our best interest for me to continue here. I think this is a good time for you to buy me out."

There was a moment of pause and then Laney threw her two cents into the conversation. "We're so excited. We're opening a chain of nightclubs with male entertainment. It's all the rage now, you know!"

Kamaya smiled. "Is it? My, my, my!" she said facetiously.

"Paxton has done so much to build your business," Laney continued. "It's time he invested that time and energy into building something for himself. I'm sure you understand."

Kamaya shifted her eyes toward Paxton who looked like he wanted to find a large hole to crawl into. For a brief second she actually felt sorry for him, and then she didn't.

"You'll be missed, Paxton. But I understand and I wish you only the very best.

"Really?" A hint of surprise rang in his tone.

"Yes! We've had a great ride together. When I started this and you agreed to come on board you were invaluable to me. I've appreciated everything you've done for me and you know I have much love for you. But if you feel it's time for you to move on, then all I can do is wish you well and keep you in my prayers."

He gave her a smile, looking as if there were more he wanted to say, but Laney spoke for him.

"So there won't be any problems with you buying out his interests? You won't hold up his cash? Because we'll need it to get our company off the ground."

Kamaya gave the woman a look before she answered. "No, none at all. In fact, I was prepared for this. The attorneys are waiting to go over the paperwork with you. Our original agreement gave you thirty percent interest in the company, and over the years you've borrowed very heavily against that. If I'm not mistaken, the final tally has you actually owing The Michelle Initiative, but they have all those figures, as well. And I have no problems working out a payment plan for what you owe."

"Thirty percent! Paxton, I thought you owned half this company?" Laney's smug expression twisted harshly.

"Laney, please," he hissed between clenched teeth. "We'll talk about it later."

"So, we won't be getting any cash?" she persisted.

Paxton squeezed his eyes shut, fighting to not blow a gasket.

Kamaya stood up. "Good luck with your future plans," she said, as she pointed them both toward the door.

"Kamaya, I…" he started, suddenly looking like he'd just lost his best friend.

"Let's go, Paxton. We need to talk to that attorney!" Laney snapped.

"Go, Paxton," Kamaya said. As he turned, she called out his name.

"Yes?"

"You really should explain the noncompete clause in your contract to Laney. I'd hate for her to be disappointed."

Laney looked from her to him and back. "What is she talking about?"

He blew a heavy sigh. Looking at the frustration painted all over Paxton's face, Kamaya answered for him.

"It means that Paxton won't be opening any night clubs with male entertainment that cater to a female clientele. At least, not in the next fifty years."

"And what if he does?" Laney snapped.

"Then I will shut you down and keep him tied up in litigation for as long as it takes."

"You wouldn't!" Laney said, her tone snarky.

Kamaya laughed. "Girl, bye! You better ask your boyfriend about me."

As Laney stomped out the door, Paxton paused, turning to meet her stare. His eyes were glazed as he fought back a flood of tears.

"I'm really sorry, Kamaya," he said softly.

Kamaya nodded. "So am I, Paxton. But I really do wish you the very best. Please make sure you leave your keys with Virginia."

Laney screamed from the outer offices. "Paxton! Let's go!"

* * *

An hour later Kamaya had shed her last tear. Paxton's personal possessions had all been packed up, moved out of his office and handed over to a delivery service to be dropped off at his home address. She'd gotten a report from the attorneys and she knew that Paxton had signed the papers that legally terminated their business arrangement.

She would miss her friend, she thought, but she knew it was past time to weed out what had become toxic in her life and let it all go. A knock on her office door drew her attention. She looked up just as Wesley poked his head through the entrance.

"Is this a good time?" he asked.

Kamaya smiled, moving onto her feet. "It's always a good time for you," she said. She moved around the desk to meet him, throwing herself into his arms.

"It's going to be okay," he whispered softly. As she clung to him, her tears returned.

"I didn't even get a chance to try and talk him out of it," she said. "He brought Laney and there was no talking any sense to him."

Wesley nodded. "Maybe that's why he brought her. Maybe he didn't want you to try and talk him out of it," he said.

She pondered his comment briefly.

"So, did you give my proposition any more thought?" she asked.

Wesley nodded. "I did and I admit it. I like the idea. It has potential."

She rolled her eyes. "It's perfect."

"I don't know about all that, now!" he teased, as he leaned in to kiss her lips.

During their late-night conversation Kamaya had broached the subject of him partnering with her in business as well as personally. He'd been receptive to the idea and they'd both agreed to sit down with their legal teams to hammer out an agreement that would work for them both. Wesley had only wanted to insure that he be allowed to bring the necessary capital to the table so that no one could accuse him of trying to take advantage of her.

When she had called to tell him about her encounter with Paxton, he'd heard the sadness that had weighed heavily in her tone. Wanting to wipe away that dejection had been foremost in his mind as he'd crossed town to get to her.

"Do you really want this, Kamaya?" he questioned, staring down at her. "If you're not ready, I need you to say so," he whispered.

Kamaya blessed him with the prettiest smile. She responded by pulling him to her, her mouth dancing the sweetest two-step against his. "I want this more than I want anything else," she said, whispering the words over his tongue.

Wesley wrapped himself around her as he hugged her even closer. "Then let's go do this," he said. "Because I really want you to be my wife."

Shortly after noon, Wesley and Kamaya stood before Reverend Tony Talevera in the French Quarter Wedding Chapel and exchanged their wedding vows. The ceremony was over in under twenty minutes. Maitlyn stood up for her sister and Kendrick arrived just in time to be Wesley's best man. His parents and hers were also there to celebrate with them.

Kamaya couldn't hold back her tears when Wesley pulled the most gorgeous ring from his pocket. A two-carat diamond was encircled by a row of high quality, French-cut, Colombian emeralds. The emeralds were surrounded by a row of round diamonds. It was stunning and sheer perfection, and everything about it screamed her name. It couldn't have been more perfect if she had picked it out for herself.

When she cried, the other women cried with her. When it was all said and done, Kamaya's only regret was agreeing to let her mother host a reception for them weeks later, when all of her family and their friends could fly in to be there. Now, she just wanted to enjoy the beauty of being married to the most incredible man in the world. She had no need of the fanfare, and Wesley only wanted what she wanted.

After a quick champagne toast and ten minutes of good wishes from her mother and his, they headed back to the office, work pulling them both back to what they loved almost as much as they loved each other.

Wesley nuzzled his face in her hair. They had been home for a while, both unwinding after another very long day. His parents had left right after the ceremony and they were both grateful for the quiet. Their dinner conversation had been a discussion of more plans and future promises. Laughter had been abundant and the wealth of joy between them had been magnanimous.

After a dinner of baked chicken and salad, and quick showers to rinse away the day, they lay together in front of the gas fireplace trading easy caresses.

"Are you happy, Wesley?" Kamaya asked, her body folded against his. Wesley responded by pulling her to him, his mouth gliding like silk against hers. He took a deep breath, inhaling her scent. He ran the tip of his nose up and down the side of Kamaya's neck, then did the same with his lips and then his fingers. Goose bumps rose against Kamaya's damp skin as he teased her feminine spirit. His kisses became more and more intense as he gently sucked on her neck, his teeth lightly grazing her throat until the tiniest marks began to rise on her flesh. She was his and he had marked her, possessively staking his territory.

Kamaya gasped, air catching in her chest as she began to grind her pelvis against the rigid hardness rising like a phoenix between his legs. She reached her hands around his torso and raked her nails down the length of his back. It was the sweetest pleasure and most delightful pain and he arched his back as a wave of electricity coursed up the length of his spine. Continuing her trek, her hands snaked down to the firm globes of his behind, squeezing and kneading the taut flesh.

Her touch was intense, and every muscle in Wesley's body ached with wanting her. He lifted his body from hers and moved to the dresser and the toiletry bag that rested atop the surface. He pulled a condom from the side pocket of the leather case and tore the cellophane pack open with his teeth. Moving back to the bed he handed the prophylactic to Kamaya who rolled the rubber over his protruding member. Dropping his body back down against hers, Wesley drew a slow path against her skin as he kissed her stomach, sinking his tongue into the deep well of her belly button.

She was gyrating unabashedly as he kissed his way back to her breasts, suckling one and then the other, then biting the skin beneath her chin, until he reached her mouth and kissed her. His tongue darted back and forth with hers. She gasped as he eased himself between her thighs, using his knees and body to pry her legs open. Kamaya gasped loudly, calling his name over and over again as he eased himself into her, dropping himself deep into her most sacred place. Wesley pressed his mouth back to hers. "I love you, Mrs. Walters," he whispered against her lips. "I love you."

Tears misted Kamaya's eyes. There was no need for words, the emotion caught deep in the wealth of energy that filled her spirit. She choked back the sobs that obstructed her voice. She loved him. More than she'd ever imagined possible. She loved him and every fiber of her being wanted to tell him, and so she answered him with her tongue, and her touch, and the easy caress of her body against his.

Wesley slowly eased the length of himself into and out of her. Moisture dripped past his thick lashes, mingling with the tears that streamed over Kamaya's cheeks. The moment was surreal, the magnitude of the experience sweeping sensations through them that neither had ever experienced before. The temptation was pleasing as his mouth locked to hers, his breath kissing her breath. Kamaya lifted her hips and welcomed Wesley home. It was ecstasy and the Promised Land and Eden, promising them both more than either could ever again want. It was bliss.

* * * * *

She frowned. *Who in the world...?* As if sensing her scrutiny, he opened his eyes and pushed up from the chair. Faith blinked. He was even taller than she originally thought, well-built and easily the most handsome man she'd seen in a long time.

"Hey," he said softly.

"I thought I dreamed you."

His deep chuckle filled the room. "No. I'm very real."

Faith tried to clear the cobwebs from her mind. "You helped me when I crashed." She thought for a moment. "Brandon?"

He nodded. "How are you feeling?"

"Everything hurts. Even breathing hurts." She closed her eyes briefly. "Um...what time is it?" she murmured.

Brandon checked his watch. "A little after eleven."

"You've been here all this time?"

"For the most part. I brought your stuff and I didn't want to leave it with anyone without your permission." He placed them on the tray.

"Thank you."

"Do you want me to call your husband or family?"

Faith wanted to roll her eyes at the husband reference, but just the thought made her ache, so she settled for saying "I'm not married."

"What about family—Mom, Dad?"

The last person she wanted to talk to was her mother. "My parents don't live here," she added softly. She had been on her way to her father's house, but chickened out before arriving and had turned around to go back to the hotel when she'd had the accident.

A frown creased his brow. "You don't have anyone here?"

"No. I live in Oregon. I just got here yesterday."

"Hell of a welcome."

"Tell me about it," she muttered.

"Well, now that I know you're okay, I'm going to leave. I'll stop by to see you tomorrow to make sure you don't need anything." Brandon covered her uninjured hand with his large one and gave it a gentle squeeze.

Despite every inch of her body aching, the warmth of his touch sent an entirely different sensation flowing through her. The intense way he was staring at her made her think he had felt something, as well.

"I…um…" Brandon eased his hand from hers. "Get some rest." However, he didn't move, his interest clear as glass. After another moment he walked to the door, but turned back once more. "Good night."

"Good night." Faith watched as he slipped out the door, her heart still racing. Her life seemed to be a mess right now, but knowing she would see Brandon again made her smile.

Don't miss GIVING MY ALL TO YOU
by Sheryl Lister, available May 2017
wherever Harlequin® Kimani Romance™
books and ebooks are sold.

Get 2 Free Books,

Plus 2 Free Gifts—

just for trying the Reader Service!

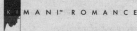

There's no mistaking the real thing

Bridget Anderson

The Only One for Me

Running the shop at her family's B and B offers Corra Coleman a fresh start after her unhappy marriage—and a tantalizing temptation in the form of millionaire Christopher Williams. With Corra's ex trying to win her back, can Chris show her how love is supposed to be?

COLEMAN HOUSE

Available April 2017!

"Humor, excitement, great secondary characters, a mystery worked throughout the story and a great villain all make Anderson's latest an especially strong book." —*RT Book Reviews* on *HOTEL PARADISE*

HARLEQUIN®
™ www.Harlequin.com

KPBA495

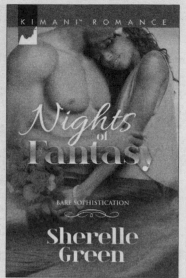

Melody of desire

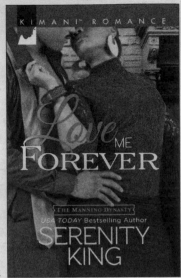

SERENITY
KING

Attorney Jarred Manning gets what he wants. Now his father's corporation has acquired a company with issues only the former owner's daughter can fix. But Nevealise Tempest is rejecting all of his proposals, for both business and pleasure… If she surrenders to passion, can she trust that he'll stick around?

{ THE MANNING DYNASTY }

Available April 2017!

www.Harlequin.com

KPSK496

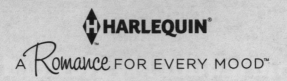

JUST CAN'T GET ENOUGH?

Join our social communities
and talk to us online.

You will have access to the latest
news on upcoming titles and special
promotions, but most importantly,
you can talk to other fans about your
favorite Harlequin reads.

Harlequin.com/Community

Facebook.com/HarlequinBooks

Twitter.com/HarlequinBooks

Pinterest.com/HarlequinBooks